CHRYSTAL VAUGHAN

CONSPIRACY OF RAVENS

Judgment comes on deadly wings...

CONSPIRACY
OF
RAVENS

Chrystal Vaughan

For my husband, Caleb

Cover Art:

Emily Valentine; copyright 2014. Stock photo provided by Emily Hershey, copyright 2014.

Maps courtesy of DreamsTime. The Tarot Card images used in this book are from the Rider-Waite-Smith deck, published in 1909, and therefore are now public domain and part of the creative commons.

Publisher's Note:

This is a work of fiction. All names, characters, places, and events are the work of the author's imagination.
Any resemblance to real persons, places, or events is coincidental.

Solstice Publishing - www.solsticepublishing.com

Copyright 2014 Chrystal Vaughan

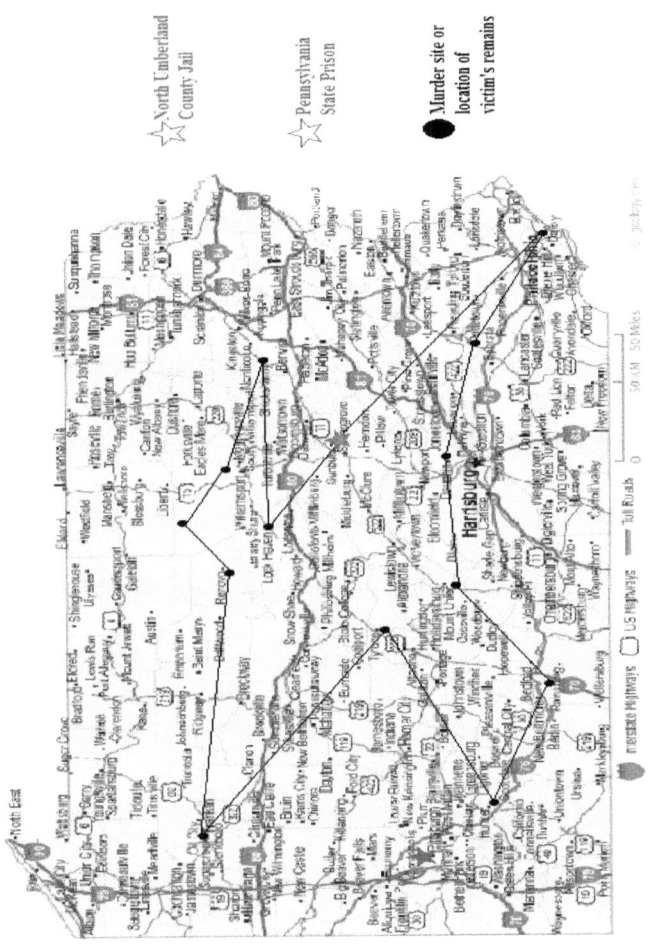

Map of Catherine Meara's murders or body recovery locations

"Although the most acute judges of the witches and even the witches themselves were convinced of the guilt of witchery, the guilt nevertheless was non-existent. It is thus with all guilt."

-Friedrich Nietzsche

"No true Witches today practice human sacrifice, torture, or any form of ritual murder. Anyone who does is not a Witch, but a psychopath."

-Starhawk

"We may brave human laws, but we cannot resist natural ones."

-Jules Verne

0-The Fool

It was a brightly sunlit day when Catherine Meara, the 'Raven Witch Killer', passed through the front doors of the Pennsylvania State Penitentiary. For a few moments, she was able to tilt her head toward its warmth and revel in its light upon her prison-paled skin. I watched her bask in its glory, her stride slow, her arms swinging at her sides. Her hair gleamed like living fire, no longer dulled to the color of old blood under the harsh fluorescent lights of captivity.

The ravens waited for her, seventeen in all, perched atop the old fashioned gates that separated the land of freedom from the realm of the depraved. They watched her approach, obsidian eyes flat in spite of the brightness of the day.

She saw them, a guard said later. She saw them there, waiting, and smiled.

One of them cawed, a harsh sound unsuited to sunlight, more closely attuned with shadows and gloom. As if it were a signal--and perhaps it was--the others raised up on clawed feet, beating their wings against the air. The terrible sound of all their feathers straining against the wind caused both gate guards to clasp their hands to their ears. I could see them from my post just inside the entrance, though the thick glass protected me from their funeral noise.

We lost eleven minutes of our lives that day. Time we cannot reclaim, though in light of what we were witness to, in light of what was lost, eleven minutes seems a paltry sum.

Officially, prisoner number 0116152 died of natural causes. A justifiable death, one might say.

I was there from the beginning to the end, from the moment Catherine entered our sphere of knowledge until the time her physical body left us behind. There was nothing natural about the Raven Witch Killer's death, or her life for that matter. We never told anyone the whole story, those of us who bore witness to her tale, those who remain, until now, that is.

They're back, you see. The ravens.

I can be silent no longer.

1-The Magician

I first heard of Catherine Meara from my boss at the Philly Herald.

"Sophia, you ever go to school with this broad?" He threw a packet of papers and photographs carelessly onto the scarred surface of my desk. In the blue glow of my computer monitor's light, Catherine's mug shot appeared to be screaming at me, eyes glowing like a demon. I dropped my half full coffee cup onto the threadbare puke green carpet and pushed myself as far back as my rolling chair could go before the carpet's wrinkles gummed its wheels.

"What the fuck?"

My boss frowned at my use of language. Rick Halpern prided himself on hiring reporters who had a handy grasp of vernacular, but a mouth like a sailor wasn't quite what he had in mind when he'd hired me. He scowled deeper at me when I was unrepentant. I gathered my wits and returned to my desk. I could see now that the woman in the photo was not screaming as I'd first imagined. Her face possessed a serene expression instead, as if we were girlfriends sharing a secret. I picked up the mug shot photo and studied it in better light, searching for something recognizable in her features.

She had bright red hair, very long and curly from what I could see in the photo. Mug shots were not always the best source of a person's appearance, lacking a certain animation, a trueness that doesn't translate on film under poor lighting and poorer circumstances. Her eyes were light in color, that I could tell, but what color--blue, green?--was unclear. Her features were regular, pleasant, and unfamiliar.

"No, I don't know her. Why, should I?"

"You both came from the same podunk town. What's it called? Potter? Potts? Pot-something. You're gonna pretend you know her, at any rate, and get an exclusive. You leave tomorrow."

I glared at him, unconcerned that, at 6'4" and 250 lbs. he out massed me by over half. "The hell I am! I'm not done with the Cortez story!"

"Phillips is taking Cortez. I want you on this. The cops are calling this woman the 'Raven Witch Killer' and I want you to find out why. As a member of the same fair sex, you are my in."

"Phillips can't write a kid's story! And I got news for you, Rick, women don't like other women."

"I don't care. You're doing this, Sophia. Do a good job, and good things will come your way. Do a piss-poor job, and you're on the Entertainment column for a month. *Capisce?*"

"You're not Italian, asshole," I muttered.

"I'm sorry, what was that? You said, 'Yes, sir, Mr. Halpern, I'll get right on that for you'-- right? 'Cause I may have misheard you...'"

"Give me my plane ticket you misogynist pig," I growled at him. Rick could be an ass but he sold me a good pitch on my future with the Philly Herald. Fresh out of journalism school, high on my escape from coal country, living it up in the big city...I was easy prey. Three years later and I was still waiting for the big story that would launch me into the big time. This could very well be my chance, but I hated the thought that Rick might be on to something. He was just so smug about it. Still...if the cops already named this criminal, given her a nickname of their own, chances were good she'd done something pretty awful. If I did a good job with this story, well, Rick was right. It would prove I was ready to take over some of the big time reporting jobs. First crack at a story was a big deal to me.

He saw his triumph in the realization I wore like a prayer shawl. He handed me my plane ticket--coach, of course--and said, "Report by phone tomorrow with a two-hundred-word intro. We'll run this as a series until you get your feet under you and give me an angle. And, Soph?--I mean it. You'll be rewarded if you take this and run. So do your best. Okay?"

"I always do my best."

In addition to my plane ticket, he gathered up the manila folder with the papers and photos and handed them to me. At home, I tucked them in my carry on as I packed, anticipating at least a week's stay.

My contact at the State Pen was one Officer Shaw. His photo was included in my packet of info, a bland state ID police shot nearly as bad as a mug shot, which revealed a younger man with sandy hair and blue eyes. A handsome face, I decided, studying his picture on the plane. Possibly a broken nose at some point, which lent it character. *Before the job, or because of the job?* I wondered.

My folder contained few stark details about the Meara case, which frankly piqued my curiosity rather than satisfying it. I'm ashamed of that curiosity, now.

Catherine Meara's vitals told me she was twenty-seven years old, my age, from Pottsdown, Pennsylvania, also where I was from. There were no listed previous or current addresses or next of kin. She was described as five foot seven inches in height and weighed one hundred and thirty-five pounds She had numerous scars and tattoos listed, that was interesting. None were visible from her mug photo and photographs of these markings were not included in my brief file. Only a typed list told me anything:

Left wrist-pentagram tattoo, black ink.
Right wrist-pentagram burned into flesh
Middle back-tree tattoo, possible occult design, multi-colored extending from right breast to left breast-

palms/hands tattoo, occult/cabalistic symbols and words inscribed on them, black ink

From left shoulder to right shoulder-bird shapes, various poses, seventeen total, black ink

The list went on like that for half a page. *The woman's body must be completely covered in scars and tattoos*, I thought. In the back of my small sheaf of papers, finally the crux of Catherine Meara's case and my purpose in visiting her was revealed, written in cop lingo.

"Suspect arrived at police HQ requesting to speak with a detective and reporter. Suspect claimed she'd murdered seventeen people and needed to confess in order 'to achieve the next level.' Suspect was not taken seriously at first but Detective Dayle Wirth took suspect's statement. Detective Wirth became shaken by the suspect's demeanor, claiming the suspect was 'a witch' and 'knew things she couldn't possibly know.'

Further questioning revealed suspect refused to speak with Detective Wirth, claiming he would 'die in the line of duty within the year.' Detective Lena Burke took over the interrogation at this point. Suspect would only tell Detective Burke, 'the girl you are all looking for here in Sunbury? The teenager who never made it home from school a couple months ago? You know the one. Brown hair, brown eyes. Neve something, I think. Ringing any bells?' Detective Burke indicated the suspect should continue, providing information on the girl's, Neve Ramirez, whereabouts if she possessed said information.

Suspect was placed in a holding cell after refusing to speak more, citing she would 'only talk to the right people. You get me to them.' Detective Burke advised suspect withholding information on a missing person's case was a punishable offense. Suspect began laughing. Detective Burke advised superiors the suspect should be remanded to State custody. Suspect was transferred to Pennsylvania State Penitentiary. Officer Bradley Shaw was informed by the suspect she would 'only confess the seventeen murders' she committed to him and a reporter by the name of Sophia Pascale from the Philly Herald. Suspect is being held at Pennsylvania State Penitentiary in solitary/lockdown until her demands can be met."

The notation continued a bit, citing details about Catherine's intake into the Pennsylvania penal system but I sat numbly in my uncomfortable plane seat, eyes seeing nothing and my penlight pointed at the shuttered plane window. That rat bastard! I thought. That's why Rick asked if I'd known her. The town and our age was secondary. She'd asked for me by name.

I flipped back through the pages, but I'd missed nothing. There was no detailed account of her crimes there, nothing for me to go on, no jumping off point to begin my questions. For the first time since I began covering homicide stories, I didn't know where to start.

I was fairly new at my job, sure, only three years as a real reporter under my belt. And my small role with the Herald didn't land me first dibs on the murderers. In fact, most of my interviews were with the more experienced reporters who had spoken to the degenerates. Only once had I interviewed a murderer myself, and that was Silvio Cortez, at the end of his twelve year stint in the California Correctional for a murder he committed while on PCP. He was *saved* now, he'd told me. I was as safe with him as a newborn kitten. And I believed him, actually. He was a shell, awaiting reentry into the atmosphere of society, doomed to burn up in its ozone.

I clicked off my penlight and returned my file to my bag. Tomorrow, after I checked in to the no doubt seediest motel Pittsburgh had to offer thanks to my cheapskate scumbag boss, I'd compose a list of possible questions and a series of sub questions to ask Catherine Meara. I took comfort in the fact that the handsome, sturdy looking

Officer Shaw would be there with me. Hey, a girl could look, right?

Before an uneasy sleep claimed me, I wondered idly why they were calling her the Raven Witch Killer. Must have had something to do with her tattoos, I guessed. I gave in to the deep, dreams of plummeting airplanes borne magically aloft by leagues of black birds, led by a flame haired woman riding a broom, laughing defiantly at the wind swept sky.

2-The High Priestess

We awoke some time later, we bleary-eyed zombies of travel. Like cattle, we disembarked but like dandelion seeds, we scattered onward to separate and unknown destinations.

I rented a car in a stupor, feeling unrested from my dream-filled slumber on the plane. I plugged in the address to the hotel on my phone's GPS and followed the mechanical woman's instructions like an obedient child. I was pleasantly surprised to find that my hotel was a modest and comfortable one, from a well-known chain, instead of some dive that rented rooms by the hour. One point for Rick.

I checked in and dragged my bags to my room. I didn't put anything away but managed to set my phone's alarm feature for two hours hence. Rick would be pissed I didn't check in but what the hell, I hadn't even talked to Catherine Meara yet and besides, he deserved it for not telling me she'd asked for me specifically.

I woke later to the insistent sound of the alarm. I took a nice long soak in the tub and dressed in a pair of black slacks and a pale blue blouse. I slipped on my sensible pumps and a dressy jacket, grabbing my purse and hotel key on my way out. I dialed Rick's cell phone in the elevator, knowing he was likely at home relaxing at eight p.m. on a Monday, the paper put to bed early during the week. I hope I ruined his communion with the whiskey bottle. I was still ticked.

Rick answered with, "Where the fuck have you been, Sophia?"

"Thanks for the decent hotel, Halpern. The roaches let me shower first. It's a real nice joint."

"Whatever. Did you talk to her yet? I want those two hundred words you owe me for tomorrow's paper, which by the way, you didn't get to me on time. Now it will have to go in Wednesday. I hope you're happy."

"I'm not happy. I haven't even seen her yet. And why didn't you tell me Catherine Meara asked for me by name? Slip your mind?"

"Don't bust my balls, Soph. It's not like I kept it from you on purpose, I just didn't have time, okay?"

"Bullshit, Rick! I would never have agreed to this if I knew some psychopathic bitch from hell had asked for me personally!"

"Well, now you have a chance to find out what she wants from you, don't you? Two hundred words, Sophia, by noon tomorrow, understand?" and he hung up the phone before I could scream at him some more.

I treated myself to a very expensive dinner on Rick's dime. Petty, I know, but I was reduced to such tactics in lieu of further confrontation. Back in my room, I turned on the television and dialed the volume down low. Changing into my pajamas, I decided to help myself to the wet bar and had a little mini-mimosa: sample sized Brut champagne and itty bitty orange juice. I piled all the pillows in the middle of the bed's headboard and leaned against them, my legal notepad in my lap and my drink close at hand. I figured Catherine would have her lawyer present, and I needed to have a few questions written in several different ways. Wording was key here. If I asked a question her lawyer objected to, I had to be clever enough to get the answer to the question by asking it in a roundabout way. I tapped my pen against my upper lip while I thought. Finally, I scribbled down a list of twenty or so questions with alternate phrasing on each. I was nervous, inexplicably, to meet with Catherine Meara. I'd never been nervous to interview anyone before, not even Cortez. But of course, none of my previous interviews had been with a self-confessed serial killer. I set my notepad on the nightstand and downed my cocktail. Though it was still relatively early, I shut off the light and laid back against the bank of pillows. I left the television on, muted, a night light against the dark unknown shadows of the hotel room.

The alcohol buzzed pleasantly through me, lulling me into a light sleep that was broken repeatedly in the night by dreams of enormous black birds, sharp beaks dripping with blood and gore.

I was groggy the next morning, awakened by my faithful phone. I'd forgotten to set the alarm but Rick was apparently not taking chances. With a groan, I noticed it was only six a.m. His payback for interrupting his nightly date with the hooch, no doubt. I didn't bother to answer. Instead, I put the extra time to good use, doing some light yoga poses to wake up my weary bones and get my blood flowing. I showered and dressed in a professional outfit consisting of a black pencil skirt, white button-down blouse, and black tailored vest. I slipped on my trusty black pumps and twisted my long dark hair into a French knot on the nape of my neck. After applying light make up, I proclaimed myself ready and stuffed everything I thought I would need into my briefcase. I grabbed my purse, long black woolen coat, and leather gloves, setting off in search of coffee and breakfast. It was not quite eight a.m. and my appointment at the prison was not for another hour, so I hit a coffee shop close to the hotel and enjoyed the morning paper over a latte and croissant. All of the nervousness I felt yesterday was oddly dissipated, but I was grateful for that. I didn't want to face Catherine Meara without all of my faculties in working order, dulled by fear.

Finally, I began the journey toward my destiny. I loaded the address of the Pennsylvania State Penitentiary into my GPS and made it there in less than twenty minutes. Its imposing edifice loomed over the sparse rolling hills of the Pennsylvania winterscape. Spring was just around the corner, a month or two away, but the treeless countryside around the premises was barren of life, still held in the crushing grip of winter's deep freeze. The enormous structure sprawled across several acres, surrounded by mile after mile of twelve-foot-tall chain link fencing, topped with razor sharp Constantine wire that curled along the upper edges of the fence like a lock of hair on a curling iron. *It's pretty typical of a State Penitentiary*, I thought, based on countless movies I'd seen. It was not too much different than the one I'd visited Cortez at, upon first glance. On my approach, however, I could see one of Pennsylvania State Pen's distinguishing features: the main gate. It was an old-fashioned affair, made of black wrought iron, topped with wicked spikes but strangely decorative below their arrow sharp tips. Its double entrance was flanked on either side by massive concrete pillars and a stone pediment above. A plain black speaker box thrust out from the ground, sitting politely on the left side of my rental car, a white button its only feature.

I pressed the button, expecting a voice to emerge, but instead, the massive gates sprang apart and began to swing ponderously inward. I eased forward, slowly making progress down a neatly graveled road. I looked behind me in the rearview mirror and saw guards stationed on either side of the gates, watching me as they swung shut again, locking me in on the state prison grounds. Neither guard was smiling. I saw their portals then, on either side of the gate, housed in the concrete pillars where the video surveillance equipment was kept no doubt. The guards would be able to see anyone who was approaching for several miles, I imagined. It was also probably cold and quite unpleasant to many spend hours in. No wonder they looked so unhappy.

I continued along the gravel road as it gently rounded a small water feature in the front of the prison's entrance. Chiseled into the stone above the entryway was the name of the place: Pennsylvania State Penitentiary, and a bronze plaque to the right of the double wooden entry doors informed me that it had been 'Established in 1829'. A tall man with sandy blond hair in a policeman's uniform was standing on the steps, waiting for me I presumed. Officer Shaw. I could tell from his photo, which portrayed him mostly accurately. I snatched my briefcase and purse from the passenger's seat and stuffed the car keys in the latter. I headed toward the steps, removing my gloves to shake Officer Shaw's hand. He had a firm grip, but not crushing like many men. He was very handsome in person, so different from his identification photo in my file, but I thought I detected something in his expression which put me off for a moment until I recognized it: relief. Officer Shaw was relieved to see me. A hint of my former trepidation returned upon this revelation. What sort of monster did he have inside this monument of stone and glass?

"Ms. Pascale, it's nice to meet you," he told me, his earnest baritone an auditory oxymoron. "Come right on inside and we'll get started. We'll need a few signatures from you and we'll get you photographed for a temporary visitor's badge, you know, standard operating procedures and all that. "

I kicked into 'reporter mode'. This I could do in my sleep. I gave Shaw my best smile and replied, "Lay on, Macduff."

He grinned back, transforming his face from handsome to downright drool-worthy. "A literature buff, huh?"

"A girl needs her hobbies, Officer Shaw."
"Call me Brad."
"And I'm Sophia."

He nodded and held the door open for me. Hmm; chivalry's not dead after all, I thought.

He led the way down a long white corridor,

explaining the history of the prison and its layout as we went. "This place was built, as I'm sure you saw, back in the late 1820's. It's kind of a rat's nest, the way they decided to lay it out. Or as we sometimes call it, the Octopus. Down this main hallway are the administrative offices, intake, processing, all that kind of thing. Also, the office of yours truly." This was said with a small, proud smile and a nod toward a closed mahogany door bearing a brass nameplate which indeed said 'Bradley Shaw'. He continued the tour. "In the center of the building is our main work area, where all the paperwork and daily schedules are handled. We call it 'the hub'."

My heels clacked on the ancient tiles of the floor as we made our way through the main hallway toward the hub. "From here, the place is just like a giant octopus, each hallway branching off of the hub. The 'arms' are designated with a letter. Arms A and B, for instance, are general population. Arms C, D, and E are lockdowns, lifers and solitary confinement cells are down that way. Arms F and G are infirmary and cafeteria areas. Arm H is where we keep prisoners who are on death row or awaiting extradition; the worst of the worst. Each arm ends in a yard for exercise. We can open up the yards and combine them, such as in general population areas, or we can keep them separate, if needed. The inmates are on a rotating schedule anyway, so we never have too many outside at one time. And that's basically it. For your visit, we went ahead and set up a table and chairs in Catherine Meara's cell. Safer to keep her in there, in my opinion. She'll be cuffed, shackled, and bolted to the floor. I must insist I or another officer accompany you into the cell while you are interviewing her. One of us will always be stationed by the door. The other officers started calling her the Raven Witch Killer, and they have good reason so caution is vital in this situation. Your well-being is my priority. Any questions so far?"

"Why Raven Witch Killer? What is the purpose behind calling her that?"

"Everyone here is terrified of her. First of all, she's the only woman we've ever had in here, except administrative staff and a few officers. No female inmates, until now. Her supposed crime is pretty horrible, if she actually did kill the girl who went missing out of Sunbury like she hinted. Crimes against children are not viewed well, even among prisoners. As for the rest of it, I'd prefer to tell you after you've spoken with her the first time. Let's get those papers signed so we can get started. I'm eager to get her out of my prison as soon as possible."

I signed round after round of papers in Shaw's office, and had my picture taken by a long-faced young woman who assured me that my badge would be ready before I left. I thanked her, and followed Shaw back to Arm H. He paused and asked, "Are you ready?

I smoothed my skirt and nodded. He wasn't exactly buoying my confidence with his statements about Catherine but what the hell, it was now or never.

"One last thing. No passing anything to her. Pens, pencils, papers, etc. And I'll be right there with you the whole time. You're going to be fine. Okay?"

I nodded stupidly again. He'd led me down Arm H to the very last cell on the right, near a barred glass door leading to what appeared to be a tiny fenced yard. The cell door was metal, black, with a small window slit approximately eye level. I'd seen a million doors like it in the movies and on TV, but never imagined I'd find myself standing in front of one, my heart beating so hard I could feel it in my fingertips.

Officer Shaw produced a key ring and selected the proper one from his collection. He nodded to the deputy standing guard to the left of the door, and placed the key into the keyhole, turning it so the tumblers made a clanking racket as they ground metal against metal. He swung the door outward, holding it open for me. His eyes caught mine and we gazed at one another for a moment, frozen in time, like two people who have just realized they are stranded together in the desert. He had a small scar across the bridge of his nose, almost between his dazzling blue eyes. A hint of five o'clock shadow traced his almost delicate jawline, lending masculinity to his nearly pretty face. What the hell? I never reacted to men this way. *Get a grip*, Sophia! I told myself.

With supreme effort, I broke eye contact first and stepped toward the woman whose story would change my life forever.

3-The Empress

Catherine was housed in a standard prison cell for the Pennsylvania State Pen. Nine feet by nine feet square, with a narrow cot bolted to one wall and a toilet and sink on the other. Aside from the table and chairs placed in the room for my interview, a single blanket was the only other thing in the room. Besides Catherine, of course.

My eyes took in the contents of the room, roaming around the starkness that filled the shadows. A single bare bulb, wrapped in a wire cage, hung suspended from the high ceiling. I was intentionally looking everywhere, anywhere but the side of the table facing the door, where Catherine Meara waited for me. I adopted a business-like manner and sat my briefcase on the table. It was a long wooden thing, the table, sturdy and beat up, with chairs to match. Shaw took up a post by the open cell door and crossed his arms, his face impassive. Only the gleam in his blue eyes betrayed his curiosity in the proceedings. I pulled my attention away from him again and sat in the empty chair waiting for me across from Catherine. Finally, I looked at her.

Catherine was a stunning beauty. Her mug shot photo had given no credence to the vibrant woman before me. Her eyes were her most arresting feature, green but with blue splotches in them. I hadn't noticed a mention in her file that Catherine had heterochromia; it simply listed her eyes as light-colored. Her hair was a living thing made of flames, mahogany, burgundy, oranges and reds colliding together and tumbling in a massive cascade of curls down her shapely back. The prison uniform, a pale washed out blue jumpsuit, complemented her skin, which was slightly dusky and not pale and freckled like that of many red-heads. Her nose was small and even, her lips were a man's dream come true, lush and full, slightly pink. I felt like a second generation Italian peasant girl in her presence. Even under the shapeless prison clothes, Catherine's flawless figure was evident and her long slender arms culminated in perfect fingers, the nails pink and pearly, clasped together on the table in front of her while she waited for me to finish my perusal of her face and form. A small smile, a Mona Lisa smile I would become so familiar with, played about her shapely lips. I smiled back in spite of myself, forgetting momentarily that she was likely a killer, and supposedly a witch.

"Hello, Sophia," her musical voice greeted me. "Thank you for coming all this way."

I lifted an eyebrow at her while rummaging in my briefcase for my voice recorder. I pulled it out and held it up. "Do you mind if I record our conversations, Ms. Meara?"

"Please, Sophia. It's Catherine. I insist."

"Very well, Catherine. I don't see a lawyer...are you sure you wish to speak to me, in the presence of Officer Shaw, without legal representation?"

"Absolutely. Again, I insist upon it."

Good enough. I turned on my voice recorder, recited the date, time and location. "Interview one with Catherine Meara, Pennsylvania State Penitentiary, February 21st, 2014. Oh and prisoner number..."

"...0116152," she finished. "Seventeen and seventeen, you know. It's so fitting. Has a nice rotundity to it, don't you think?"

I ignored this and pulled my prepared questions out of my briefcase, closing it and setting it on the floor next to my chair. Before I could begin, however, Catherine continued speaking.

"You desire him, don't you, Sophia? Tell me, how long has it been since you lay with a man?" she whispered.

I blushed but forged ahead with my first question. "So, Catherine. You asked for me to be here and so, here I am. I'd like to state, for the record, you have no lawyer present and you stated you wish to continue without legal counsel. Is that correct?"

"My lawyer has been made aware that I will be speaking with you, regardless of his spineless presence. In fact, I prefer it that way." Her tone was serious, but she still had that little smirking smile, her expression seeming to mock me for my professional tone. *See, I can play your game*, the look said, *and I can play just as good as you can.*

"Very well. Can you tell me why you turned yourself in?"

"Don't you want to know why I asked for you, Sophia?"

"No Catherine, I don't. My interests in your case are strictly professional and anything regarding your reason for including my involvement is irrelevant."

She sat back in her seat, chains clinking softly beneath the table. She was openly gloating now, wearing her triumph like a queen's crown.

"Exactly, Sophia. That is why I chose you to hear and tell my story. I remember you, though I can tell you don't remember me. We went to the same school in that ratty town, but I ran in different circles, ran with an older crowd but I felt your power even then. Before I finished my project, I'd seen your picture in the paper and remembered the taste of that power. Some article you wrote about the occult, do you remember? You wore an evil eye amulet for the photo, the same one you are wearing beneath your oh-so sensible button-down shirt, warm against your breasts. I knew you would be strong enough to resist me, to tell the story right."

"I remember the piece, of course. I'm sorry, I don't remember you from Pottsdown but I've moved on from my childhood. Your other comments about my supposed 'power', well, I hate to disappoint you but I'm just an ordinary person."

Catherine completely ignored my statement. "Your grandmother gave you that amulet, I believe. Your parents died, in a car accident supposedly, when you were nine and you lived with her until you graduated. There's something else too, another person...I can't tell who, exactly, but maybe an uncle? Someone close to you..."

"Stop!" I choked out. My blood ran cold at her words. "Anyone can find out that information. Everyone who lived in Pottsdown knew about my parents, for Christ's sake."

"This uncle, he touched you, made you do things. That's why you have so many problems with men, in fact, you're practically frigid aren't you? You'd love to spread yourself for Officer Shaw here but you won't because..."

"Shut up, SHUT THE FUCK UP!"

"...Because when a man touches you, you can only remember those dark, sweaty nights, living in terror when your uncle would come into your room, your grandmother was too blind to save you..."

The light bulb in the small cell started to flicker off and on. "Stop, please," I breathed one last time before it blew completely, sprinkling us with small specks of glass which tinkled merrily onto the surface of the table in the suddenly tomb-like darkness. I heard Officer Shaw call for back up on his radio, felt the comforting light of his standard issue flashlight on my face as he probed the room with its beam. His voice, asking me if I was okay, sounded far away. Catherine's laughter echoed in the empty chamber and insinuated itself into my brain where it set up an echo of its own.

Guided by Shaw's flashlight, I stumbled from my seat, pawing at my recorder and briefcase as I went. I sank to the floor in the hallway outside the cell, where thankfully light still reigned supreme. Catherine's voice followed me there. "I told you, Sophia. You're powerful, though you may not be a match for me like I thought. How disappointing! There's no turning back now...I choose you as the light to my darkness. Isn't it ironic?"

Other guards arrived and collected my belongings for me, Shaw offering me a hand up. He gave orders to clean the glass and replace the bulb, and to remove the table and chairs for today, locking her in for the night. I ignored his hand, outstretched toward me to help me rise and got to my feet without looking at him, instead standing awkwardly with my briefcase hanging limply from one hand and the voice recorder gripped in the other. Shaw took hold of my elbow and led me to his office. He opened the door, gesturing to the empty chair on the near side of his desk. I sank into its leather embrace gratefully and willed myself invisible.

4-The Emperor

Shaw dropped into the chair on the other side of the massive oak desk. He opened a drawer and held up a flask with a raised eyebrow, questioning my participation.

"Hell, yes." I reached for the flask and took a healthy swig of good Irish whiskey, appreciating the glow blazing a trail down my throat to warm my stomach. I pretended not to notice Shaw watching me.

"I'm impressed. And dismayed to think you might be able to drink me under the table."

I gave him a ghost of a smile and returned his flask. To his credit, he took a small sip before returning it to his drawer, rather than trying to outdrink me, to prove something. Of course, he was at work so maybe that was the real motive.

"So. Warden Ellis asked I give him a full report on today's events concerning the interview but I think there are some things I'll be leaving out," Shaw said quietly, his eyes on me while he spoke.

I was momentarily taken aback. "A warden? You mean, you're not in charge here?" I felt stupid for not realizing that.

"Well, on paper, no. Warden Ellis, however, has been with us several years and recently his golf game has been suffering egregiously under the burden of his workaday responsibilities, so in practice, you're still stuck with me."

I said nothing, actually relieved I wouldn't have to report what happened to someone else, to relive those terrible words Catherine hurled at me like daggers.

He mistook my silence for something besides relief. "Unless...you'd rather work with someone else? I can ask another officer to..."

"No! No. Our arrangement is fine."

"She does it for fun, Sophia," he said. "When she first arrived, we had an officer, Edgar Pulton was his name. Ed. He was on guard duty for her night rotation. Ed wasn't the greatest guy--don't get me wrong, he passed all of the psych tests required to work here, and was with us four years before that bird bitch got here. Still, he was kind of a douche, you know? Kind of puffed up, self-important. Liked feeling in control of people.

One night, he was on duty down Arm H, mostly to keep an eye on her. Video surveillance shows him stopping at her door and opening the hatch, talking to her apparently. No sound on those tapes, so we don't know what exactly was said. What I can say is when you watch the tape, you can see him getting more and more agitated as they spoke, until he started screaming at her door, the veins on his face and neck popping out, spraying spit everywhere. Finally, he started clawing his eyes out with his own fingernails, tearing at the flesh on his face and wiping the blood on the outside of her door."

"Dear God," I said faintly.

"He ripped out his jugular with his own fingers. Video shows him slumping to the floor, bleeding out before anyone even knew anything happened. He never radioed, and no one heard him screaming at her. By the time anyone checked on him, it was far too late. Pulton was dead in minutes anyway. And that's not all. We call her the 'Raven Witch Killer' because of the bird. He'd drawn a raven on the outside of her door in his own blood. How he managed to do that with no eyes, I couldn't tell you."

"Did she tell you what was said, why he killed himself?"

"All she would say is he got what he deserved. We took all her things away, but we got nothing else from her."

"Has she done anything else like that?" I asked.

"After we took away her paper and pencils, she stopped speaking. Until today."

"What was she writing? Did she draw anything?"

"If she did, she either flushed or ate the pages. We never saw any evidence she was using them, other than the need for a pencil sharpener and more paper," he answered. "We have surveillance cameras in her room, of course, but there are suspicious jumps and blank spots in the recordings." He shrugged, having no answer for the discrepancy.

I was silent for a moment. Then, "What she said to me. No one ever knew about any of that, with my uncle."

"Sophia, you don't have to..."

"But I do! Don't you see? How did she know any of that? I never told a soul, not even a priest at confession. If I'd told, if my grandmother found out, it would have killed her. She'd already lost her daughter. I couldn't tell her what her son was, couldn't break her heart. I just couldn't." Tears pooled over my bottom lashes and dripped from my chin to trace warm tracks down my throat.

"Most victims don't report the crimes committed against them in those cases," Shaw's gentle voice reminded me as he handed me a tissue. "As a reporter, I'm sure you're aware of the statistics in sexual abuse cases."

I mopped up my face and met his eyes. I saw concern, but not pity, and it warmed me. "My grandmother went to her grave thinking her son was a kind, caring man. He finally got what was coming to him a couple of years after her death."

"Don't tell me you hired a hit man?"

I smirked. His levity helped break the serious tension of our conversation. "Yeah, I sure did. God."

"Ah, the original murderer," he said.

"You strike me as a good Irish Catholic boy. Should you be saying such things? Am I in danger of being struck by lightning simply as a bystander?"

"I'm good, or rather I try to be. I'm Irish, true, through no fault of my own. Catholic, well that I'm not. Although, I'm questioning my lack of a belief system since she came to my prison, I'm not ashamed to tell you."

I took off my grandmother's evil eye pendant and put it in his hand. Our eyes locked again, and I said, "Keep this with you. Some things don't need your belief to do their job. Or so my grandmother told me."

He smiled and it reached all the way up into those baby blues. I returned it. Catherine was right on all accounts, I told myself. I was very attracted to Shaw. Maybe I'd even do something about it. Someday.

5-The Hierophant

"So today was a bust, I guess," Shaw lamented as he walked me to my car. "I was hoping to have something more on her than her word."

"I'm sorry I lost it in there. I let her rattle me but it won't happen again. I promise."

"I believe in you. Tomorrow morning, then?"

"I'll be here, bright eyed and bushy tailed." I took my briefcase and purse with thanks and climbed into the rental car.

Back at the hotel, I kicked off my shoes and lay fully clothed across the bed. Did I believe what Catherine said about me, about my 'power'? I didn't know what to think. My grandmother was Sicilian, very Catholic but also extremely superstitious. She was of the old country generation, where orthodox religion lived comfortably alongside pagan ritual. She told me once nearly the same thing Catherine told me today.

"*Caro*, you have the gift," she'd said.

"What gift, Nonna? A new dress?" I teased.

"The eye, honey, the eye. Not to worry, your Nonna will help you, when the time is right."

But the time never came. Nonna died when I was nineteen. I moved from Pottsdown as soon as she passed and because my grandmother saved every penny, because we'd lived so simply during my childhood, my education was paid for by her estate.

Now I had to consider the possibility both Nonna and Catherine knew something about me that I didn't. Shaw hadn't asked, assuming I guess that Catherine had broken out the light bulb or it could possibly be a coincidence. Yet I wondered. It wouldn't be the first time something broke, seemingly on its own, when I was upset or angry.

I fell asleep, though it was early afternoon, questioning my beliefs about myself and my place in the world. It was after six p.m. when I woke, hours past my deadline with Rick. I ignored my phone, knowing he was probably pretty pissed and taking it out on my cell. I fired up my laptop, and rattled off the required snippet for the paper:

"Catherine Meara sits in a nine by nine prison cell at Pennsylvania State Penitentiary, the only woman housed in the prison in its entire history. She asked, upon turning herself in to State Police Headquarters, only one officer and one reporter be present at her confession. A confession, she claims, to the murders of seventeen people. Ms. Meara is the last person one might expect to fit the profile of a serial killer. She is young, attractive, and seemingly intelligent. Additionally, most serial killers are statistically men, whereas Catherine Meara is clearly a woman.

"Ms. Meara sat, chained and shackled as I approached. A wooden table and chairs were provided by Officer Bradley Shaw for our conversation, the officer chosen by Catherine to hear her confession. Officer Shaw insisted on having armed guards present while I interviewed her. It seems Catherine Meara hasn't been the most cooperative inmate, though she chose to turn herself in.

"Catherine Meara appears to be in flawless physical health. Her body is said to be adorned with numerous occult-related tattoos and markings. On her wrists, visible in spite of the prison uniform, are two pentagrams. One is tattooed with spidery black ink, while the other appears to have been burned into her flesh like a brand. She speaks of witchcraft, and she speaks in riddles. So far her only statements are the adornments she wears with pride. It seems Ms. Meara is a true believer.

A believer of what remains to be seen."

There. Fuck Rick. Over two hundred words and he could bite me. I fired it off to him and logged off the computer. After a quick shower, I ordered a bowl of cereal from room service. The front desk advised me they had some issues with billing they needed to speak to me about. I sighed. I'm sure Rick cancelled payment on my room, payback for my late submission. I crunched my cereal in bed and decided to deal with it in the morning.

My dreams were hunters that night, stalking me with my uncle's face. Just as he covered my body with his and slapped a sweaty hand across my mouth to muffle my screams, his head transformed into a giant black raven's, its sharp beak stabbing down at me until I knew no more.

6-The Lovers

I awoke the next morning with a sleep hangover, the kind of fuzzy headed feeling that comes from repeatedly interrupted sleep. *This trip is going to be the death of me*, I thought, but quickly squashed those thoughts as flashbacks from my nightmares replayed themselves in my mind's theater.

I was running late already, so I slapped on some fresh clothes, washed up, grabbed a coffee and almond scone from the coffee shop by the hotel and hit the road.

In spite of yesterday's disaster, I had no intention of letting Catherine get to me today. Bitch was going to play my game instead. I knew a little something about what she was, too.

Officer Shaw was waiting for me on the sweeping steps of the prison entrance again. I smiled at him, happy to see him, and handed him the extra coffee I'd picked up. He thanked me profusely, and seemed genuinely touched by the small gesture.

"You're a spot of sunshine today," he observed. "Feeling better?"

"I'm ready for her this time. Let's do it!"

He handed me my badge, forgotten in the turmoil of yesterday's failure. Ignoring the tingling in my fingers as our hands touched during the exchange, I clipped the badge to my suit jacket and allowed Shaw to lead me down Arm H to Catherine's cell. Someone had replaced the bulb in the ceiling and covered the wire cage with a finer mesh wrap. In case such a thing were to happen again, I guessed. Taking no chances she would be able to fashion a weapon out of glass debris.

Catherine was once again shackled and cuffed, our same wooden table and chairs set up like before. The stage was set, with the same players. The only difference was my attitude.

Catherine clapped her hands together in delight when she saw me. Hindered by the cuffs, she nonetheless more than adequately conveyed her glee in having another crack at me.

"Good morning, Catherine," I said evenly. "Now, where were we?"

"Hell-o Sophia! Pleasant dreams last night? Tell me, was our hunky officer in any of them?"

Shaw cleared his throat, embarrassed, but said nothing. He took up his post by the door. I ignored him and concentrated on the task at hand.

"You know, I'm starting to think you might have an interest in Officer Shaw, Catherine. Are you jealous?"

Her face came alive with fury. "In his DREAMS!" she spat, nearly hissing the words, cat like. "No man touches me."

"Tsk, tsk. Sounds like I'm not the only one with uncle issues." I was baiting her on purpose, pleased to have found a chink in her armor so quickly. She realized it, too, and smoothed her features back into pleasant interest, through sheer force of will. It was like watching Claymation on those old cartoons, where the putty melted from one thing into another.

"Well done, Sophia. Are we through with the pathetic attempts to play with my psyche? Or do you want to hear some details about your parents' last moments on earth?

"Nice try, Catherine. Now...let's talk about why we are both here. You asked for me, whatever your reasons, and so here I am. As you wished it, it is so. What am I here for Catherine? What have you done?"

A sly smile slid across her lips. "I heard that Sophia. So mote it be, your mind said, though your lips spoke differently. Very well. A binding oath we will craft, you and

I. A light witch and a dark witch, as I said. I will reveal all, and you will hear my words. When I am through, you will tell the world what I have wrought. That is our pact."

"What's in it for you? Sick pleasure? All the witch crap aside, what, at your core, is your intent?"

"Judgment, Sophia. I crave only judgment."

I studied her for any tells, any clues that would betray a lie. Her face was a fortress, inscrutable, and I was swimming once again in deep waters. I reflected on her words, and in a flash, my life preserver presented itself. I changed tactics and crossed my fingers it would work.

I sat back in my chair, assuming a relaxed posture, legs crossed. I calmed my mind, emptied myself of external thoughts, quelled and tamped down my anxieties. I concentrated on slowing my heartbeat, seeking a Zen state in which to dance with this psycho.

"Okay, Catherine, you win. I'll play it your way."

I removed her mug shot photo from my briefcase. I hadn't planned to need anything other than my files so I had to improvise quickly. I untied the thin satin sash on my blouse and unthreaded it from the loops. Catherine's expression betrayed her curiosity, and she leaned forward, interested. Her features rapidly changed to horror and anger as I methodically began to wind the sash around her photograph, and intoned:

"I bind you left
I bind you right
I bind you Catherine
With all my might
I bind you now
I bind you day
I bind you night
With this bind I vow
An it harm none, save ye
So mote it be."

She sat, stunned, as I completed the binding ritual, slipping the wrapped picture into my pocket, my blouse hanging loose around me. I saw fear in her eyes and I felt a fierce bolt of triumph shoot through me. I could tell she thought she'd just witnessed me out myself as a witch, but I read as much as I could about the occult, both as a kid and for my job. I sought answers to questions Nonna left unanswered, information for news stories I wrote. I was never a true believer. I had no compunction about using it against Catherine, however. She was a true believer, I could see it swimming in her strange eyes, and I was glad that the playing field was a little more even.

"So what do you say, Catherine? Should I leave now? Or are you done fucking around?"

Her eyes turned cold, her tone brittle. Her voice rang out loud and clear, dancing around in the empty chamber. I slipped my hand in my pocket where the voice recorder lay nestled against the bound photo and clicked on the record button.

"The first two were the Lovers. I drew their card on a bright sunny day two summers ago. The Goddess had forsaken me but the dark one gathered me into his bosom and whispered all the secrets of the world into my ears. My life's goal, he said, once completed would ensure my place in his kingdom and cause my name to live forever."

"You sound like a religious wingnut zealot, Catherine. Your drama classes are showing." I had no idea if she'd taken drama classes but I calculated her sense of theatrics hadn't come from a vacuum. She glared at me, and I knew I'd hit the mark.

"Do you want to tell the story, Sophia?" she snapped.

"By all means, please continue."

She stared at me in hatred for a few minutes and then continued.

"As I said. The first two ravens were the Lovers. The dark lord has his own Tarot, did you know?"

"I did actually. However, the Lovers is part of the classic Rider-Waite deck, as I'm sure you know. And Rider-Waite has twenty-two cards in the major arcana, not seventeen, so if you're correlating your crimes to the cards you're off by a few. Your story is not matching up, Catherine. Are you a witch or a Satanist?"

"Thank you for the occult lesson, Sophia. I forgot you are the expert here. By the way, you are sadly mistaken if you think your little binding spell is going to work on me." She was haughty again, all confidence returned, smiling that irritatingly coy little smirk and cloaked in her sense of superiority. "As I'm sure you know, Wicca is a belief in balances, both light and dark. The Goddess's consort, the Green Man, is also called the Horned God. When she would not hear me, I turned to him and he has shown me my path, paved in sacrifice and blood. The Lovers card chose two sinners, two who perverted love, people who used drugs and defiled themselves, throwing the God and Goddesses gifts in their faces. Wretches whom no one would miss."

"So you are a vigilante, is that is? Taking out the poison in the world so you could buy your way into the good graces of your chosen gods?"

She completely ignored me, caught up in her own tale. "Bums. Drug addicts, the scum of the earth. Even though the Goddess has turned from me, the dark lord and I serve her, in all ways. They were an abomination to love, disgusting and offensive to the eye. Love should be beautiful.

"I found them in the forest, these lovers, fucking in the leaves under one of the Goddess's trees. Their bodies were unwashed, unwholesome. They reeked of methamphetamine, and left their trash strewn all about their campsite. The man's beard was black, bristling and ugly by the light of their campfire. I came upon them while they embraced, naked and writhing against each other.

"I prayed to the Horned God to guide my steps, to grant me silence and lead my blade to its true home. The woman was on top of the man, her fleshless body undulating like a snake. Her greasy brown hair hung down her back in a filthy curtain, swaying with her movements. Both of them were so wasted on the drug there was barely anything left of them and they appeared as two skeletons rubbing their bones against each other. I worried that they were too poor of specimens for the special sacrifice, but the dark lord whispered on the wind, light as raven's wings, assuring me they were perfect, for a start.

"I raised my dagger and crept closer, naked too, so that no whisper of cloth could betray me. They were so entwined with one another that they could not hear me. Their eyes closed in ecstasy, they did not see me. I waited until the woman's cries frightened the animals into silence, and I placed my blade at the base of her skull and pushed as hard as I could, my dark lord giving me strength, and she spasmed both in sexual release and release from her mortal coil. I knew only rapture as her hot blood spilled over my hand.

"Her man knew nothing out of the ordinary until I shoved her aside, disengaging her from his sex with a disgusting sound, taking her place on top of him but not for the sex act, no, never that. Something much more visceral, more real! Before he could gather himself, I plunged my bloody knife into his chest over and over, his blood spraying my face and breasts.

"My arms grew tired, so I ceased my hacking of his corpse. The man's eyes were open and the surprised expression on his face amused me so much I laughed aloud.

"Finally, I dragged the two of them to a small area I'd cleared of leaves. I arranged them side by side, arms around each other, foreheads touching. It was so tender, seeing them that way. I cried then, a little, and thanked them for their sacrifice. I assured them their lives were worth something, now. I cast my circle and offered them to the Horned God. He accepted, sending messengers on the air to witness this, my first act of devotion. I completed the ritual, bathed in their blood, and drew forth my own blood to complete the ritual, tracing the dark lord's raven symbol upon their chests to anoint them.

"Once the ritual was completed, I released the circle and left them there to nourish the forest and the earth with their sacrifice. I retrieved my clothing, washing the blood from my body and face the best I could with damp leaves and a jug of water I found at their campsite. I poured the rest on the fire and left that place forever, seeking out my next destination, the next place my dark lord would send me."

Catherine sat back, pleased to have released the story of her first sacrifices. I could see it excited her, as a fine sheen of sweat dampened her hairline and upper lip. She looked so pleased, so goddamn smug, I wanted to scream at her.

I was shaken, mostly, by the passion with which she told the story, the loving detail she'd given to it. There was no doubt I believed her. She was seized with a fervent desire to return to that time, to kill again. It was there, in her posture, in every fiber of her being, glowing from her body in radiant waves. She looked like a woman who'd just spent an hour on the receiving end of great pleasure. With an iron will, I stopped myself from shaking violently or curling into a ball in the corner.

"That's a fascinating story, Catherine," I finally replied, infusing as much disdain in my voice as I could muster. "Where did this supposed murder take place, I wonder, that you could just walk into the woods and walk right out?"

"You'll believe," she whispered. "You already do."

"I'll need a little more to go on than bloody dreams you had as a prepubescent teen, Catherine. How about some evidence? Tell me where to have the officers look for these bodies you say you left artfully arranged in the forest."

"Sure, Sophia, no problem."

I hid my surprise and turned to Shaw, who I noticed was looking a little green around the gills. "Officer Shaw, do you have an atlas around that Catherine and I can use?"

He cleared his throat a few times, then croaked out, "Sure, no problem," unconsciously echoing Catherine. He got on his radio to find us an atlas or map of the state.

Catherine still sat back in her chair, now humming and swinging her feet like a happy schoolchild waiting for a treat. It was unnerving, and set my teeth on edge.

After a brief wait, an officer brought a map of the state, similar to the ones you can buy at a gas station. We unfolded it on the table's surface, and I pointed to it. "Where do we start?"

She pointed to a blank spot just south of Lock Haven, a nowhere place in Clinton County nestled in the swampy area between several major waterways. With the Blue Ridge Mountains to the northwest, finding bodies would be difficult.

"We'll get some officers from Clinton County to start looking," Shaw said over my shoulder. His tone made it clear he thought the chances of finding anything were pretty slim, too.

I stood, my time with Catherine at an end for the day. I could hardly believe I'd been there so long already, could hardly believe I had to come back again to hear more of her filth. Shaw preceded me from Catherine's cell, but she called to me and I turned. "See you tomorrow!" she sang out.

I said nothing but clutched the map tighter, gripping my briefcase handle so hard my knuckles turned white. I retreated down the Arm H to the main artery with Shaw in the lead. And it was a retreat. Catherine's confession to two brutal murders affected me deeply. I felt as though the bottom of the world was a gaping maw beneath my feet, waiting to swallow me alive. People disappeared all the time, I kept thinking, and sometimes people like Catherine were the reason why.

Shaw seemed to sense I wasn't in the mood for small talk, so he ushered me into his office without a word. We sat, poring silently over the map of Pennsylvania, marking the place she'd pointed to with a red circle of ink. I felt nauseous, thinking how closely it resembled a circle of blood.

I finally broke the silence. "Did you believe her?"

"Without question. It's unfortunate she's stark raving mad. I'm sure her lawyer will play the mentally fucked up card and I really wanted her to burn. Pun intended."

"She's not, though. Not crazy in the traditional sense."

"Were you in the same room?" he said, incredulous.

"Listen, I'm no psychiatrist but I get the sense she's just messing with us. Me, in particular."

"So you don't think she did it?"

"Of course I do. I just don't think she's crazy. Crazy people don't know right from wrong. For all that she's cloaking her actions with her 'belief' about the 'dark lord' telling her to do it, I think it's a sham. She knows what she did was wrong. She's fucking with us."

"You could be right. I was just hoping she would be transferred out to a psych ward soon," he sighed.

"Hey, I've got to run and check in with my boss. He's being a pain in the ass...I'll be back in the morning for our next fun-filled installment."

He walked me to my car again. Before I could get in, he grabbed me in a spontaneous hug, and then stepped away quickly, as if worried I would slap him. I managed to keep my reaction to myself but my flesh was warm beneath my clothing everywhere he'd touched. Bemused, I got in my car and drove away. I saw him, still standing there, in my rearview mirror. He raised his hand in good-bye.

As I put the prison in my dust, I noticed two enormous ravens perched on the portico over the double entry gates. They watched me leave. I shuddered with atavistic fear, and crossed myself, switching hands on the steering wheel to then make the sign of the evil eye.

7-The Chariot

When I arrived at the prison the following morning, Shaw was nowhere to be found. I headed down the main arm of the building toward the hub, pausing to peek in his office but not finding him there.

At the bullet-proof glass encased officer's station, another uniformed officer—"Deputy Reynolds, ma'am"—escorted me to Arm H. I saw Shaw waiting halfway down and I greeted him, puzzled.

He nodded to his officer, who returned back up the arm to the Hub. Shaw led me aside, his firm, warm grip welcome on my upper arm.

"There was some excitement in the middle of the night. As a result, her lawyer is insisting he be present for any further meetings with his client, in spite of her wishes. He's an officious little prick, I'd like to…well, never mind."

"What happened?"

"One of my officers on guard duty at the main gate yesterday evening took a shot at one of those damned birds perched on the concrete on the top span. His partner said he was getting irritated with their noise, complaining they were shitting all over everything. He drew his revolver and fired a shot. As soon as he hit it, the fucking thing toppled to the ground, flapping and shrieking, while the other one dive bombed the officer who'd shot its friend, clawing and pecking at him. He started firing at the second bird, shot his partner in the leg and ended up shooting himself in the face."

"Oh, no…"

"According to matching video surveillance information, at the same time that the bird was shot, Catherine Meara began screaming in her cell. Video shows her night guard on duty backing away from her door with his hands over his ears. I don't live far, and since I'm the one in charge around here, they call me when shit hits the fan. I got here as fast as I could, came in through the side door, and was just in time to hear her screaming in there. I opened her cell and found her laying on her cot with her eyes closed, her mouth open wide and the most hellacious noise coming from her. If she has vocal chords left I'll be amazed. I radioed for a medic, but they were already on their way for the officers out front. I hadn't even heard about that yet. I hauled ass out front and sure enough, there was a fucking massacre out there. I've got the fucking warden in his office, in my prison, asking questions and everyone's on edge in this place today because of that bitch."

I gazed at his outburst, wide eyed. He ran his hands through his hair, turning it into a sandy, untidy mess. I touched his forearm, lightly. "I'm sorry Brad. About your officers, I mean."

He sighed and said, "The worst part is that those damned things are still out there on the mantel, mocking me."

"They are both still there? I thought you said your officer killed one? I didn't see either of them on my way in this morning."

"They're both there. Look at them closely before you leave today." He gave me a look I couldn't decipher out of the corner of his eye. As if I would know *how* there were still two birds...I needed to address this quickly before it got out of hand. "You don't think...I'm what she is, do you?"

"No, I do not think you are a fucked up nutcase, psycho witch bitch."

"Well that's a relief!"

"I am beginning to see why she picked you, though."

I bristled a little. "Oh?"

"You have something different than most people. You can't deny it Sophia. I think we may have need of that something, whatever it is, before it's all said and done."

"I don't know what you're talking about but I guess thanks for the vote of confidence. So–let's go face the dragon, shall we?"

I smiled at him, and he smiled back. It didn't reach all the way up to his eyes, like usual, but it something at least. "Come on," I joked. "Lawyers aren't all that bad, are they?"

He snorted. "Tell me if you still feel the same way in a few hours."

We entered the cell together. I was still feeling confident until I was introduced to the lawyer.

Ruben Maxwell looked exactly like a ferret, which is cute on a ferret but not on a human. He was short, much shorter than Shaw, with small, darting black eyes and a sharply pointed face. The lack of chin combined with his receding widow's peak only heightened the effect. Shaw introduced me to him as Ms. Pascale of the Philly Herald, as requested by his client. Maxwell's limp, damp handshake made me want to wipe my hand on my skirt but I felt doing it would be rude. I sat in my usual chair. Another had been placed beside Catherine for her ferret.

After a few minutes of listening to his nasally voice whine about how he'd been left out, and how he now demanded copies of my taped conversations with Catherine, I abandoned all compunctions I harbored about rudeness where he was concerned. I simply waited for him to wind down, then made it a point to turn on my voice recorder as ostentatiously as possible. I addressed my comments to Catherine.

"Good morning, Catherine. How are you feeling? I understand there was a disturbance last night?"

"No! No, no, no. You may not ask my client any

questions that do not pertain to the subject of her request," Maxwell interjected.

Catherine turned her head toward him, slowly, on creaking neck joints. She stared at him for long moments, unblinking, completely silent. He fidgeted, then sighed. "Fine, okay, whatever."

Catherine turned back to me. Her eyes were bloodshot, and her voice was raspy. She whispered, "Don't let them hurt the ravens anymore, Sophia. That's my job."

A chill went down my spine but I kept it together. "Sure Catherine. I'll tell them not to hurt your birds. Are you able to talk today? Do you wish to continue where we left off? You'd killed the two victims near Lock Haven, wasn't it? What happened next?"

"We *are* alike, you know," she said, ignoring my questions as usual. "You told Officer Shaw you were nothing like me, but you are. We are two sides to the same coin. Both of us orphans, raised to become witches."

I ignored her statement. She knew nothing of my grandmother. "Your parents are dead? Do you want to tell me about that? What was your childhood like, Catherine? Did it contribute to these murders?"

She gave me a cold look, her voice haughty and distant. "That's none of your business, Sophia."

"Well, Catherine, you brought it up."

"The third raven I sacrificed was a boy. An older boy, college age, not a child, but still a boy. I'm a waitress, you know. I work at a place for a while until I find a suitable sacrifice for the Horned God, and then move on. He tells me where to go, where to find them. I was waiting tables at a diner near Shickshinny when the boy came in to the restaurant and sat at one of my tables. He was a beautiful boy. Thick brown hair, slightly curled at the ends. Sea green eyes. Charming, that's what he was. He charmed me." Catherine's scream roughened voice took on a dreamy quality. "He was so pretty and I loved him, a little, as soon as I saw him. It was the love, my love for him that killed him. The dark lord is a jealous consort," she whispered, tears forming pools in her strange eyes, shimmering on her bottom lashes. "I'd wanted him so very much, you see, and then he had to die and take his beauty with him. I raged against it, vowed to the Horned God that he would not have the boy, but it was no use.

"I waited on him, took his order, and gave him special attention. I wanted his last meal to be the best. He flirted with me shamelessly, this pretty, charming young boy. Asked for my number. I said I'd go one better, and that my shift was ending in an hour. I let him know he could pick me up, if he wanted. He said he wanted.

"He returned like he promised, the poor foolish, pretty boy. His eyes were so wonderful. I wish I could have kept them. He asked me where we should go, so I suggested parking on a hill somewhere to enjoy the stars and get to know each other. He seemed surprised, this boy who surely had a way with women, but he was eager and that was all that was needed. We went parking, and he hesitated to touch me. I offered him some weed, to relax him. The drug makes them slow, easier to surprise, but he declined. I could tell he wanted to make a move on me, to touch my skin with his, but he was too scared. It was good he was afraid, for I fear what would have happened to me if I were unfaithful to the dark lord, and I would not have stopped him had he touched me.

"We talked, instead, or rather he did, nervously and for hours, his soul poured out like a pitcher of milk under a moonless sky. After a time, he said we should head back, it was getting late. I agreed, disappointed that he hadn't tried harder to fuck me. He'd tempted me with more than his immense sea colored eyes and earnest conversation.

"He tried to leave, to make his car obey his commands, but it was stuck fast. He asked me to take the wheel and he would push, thinking the car was stuck in mud or loose dirt. That was what he said, the last words he spoke.

"He got out and walked to the back of the car, an older model Honda, nothing fancy. I slid over to the driver's seat. As soon as I saw him in the rearview mirror, putting his muscular arms and back into the effort of moving the car rather than making love to me, I poured my anger into the ignition, turning over the car's engine with a roar and slamming the gearshift into reverse in one swift motion, stomping hard on the gas pedal. I felt the tires go over his body, a huge jolt that rocked the car, and I heard him scream. I put the car in drive and ran the tires over him again, the wet crunching loud enough to be heard over the engine's scream. I ran him over again and again. The Chariot was his card, and it was his sacrifice to the dark lord to let loose his blood beneath its wheels. I wept the entire time.

"Once I was sure he was dead, I got out of the car to complete the ritual. His body lay broken and mangled in the car's headlights, no longer beautiful. His skull was crushed, those wonderful eyes mutilated and oozing from their sockets. Still crying, I dragged him a little ways from the car and arranged him as though he were sleeping. I cast the circle and completed the ritual with my blood, making the raven appear on him, knowing they watched from above. I closed the circle and left him there, taking his car to carry me on my way to the next place, sobbing as I washed the blood and hair from its sides. I vowed to the dark lord that I would never be tempted again, that no man should ever touch me.

"The work of the chosen is hard, Sophia. So hard," she ended in a voice barely above a whisper and laid her fiery head down upon the table.

Maxwell sat there gaping at me. His teeth were even pointy like a weasel's. Finally, he spoke. "Jesus fucking Christ!"

"Not even remotely," was my response.

****

Maxwell and I left Catherine slumped at the table, joining Shaw at the doorway to her cell. The three of us proceeded in silence to Shaw's office, where we each grabbed a leather clad chair and sank down gratefully, as drained by the hearing of Catherine's tale as she apparently was by the telling of it.

I was the first to break the quiet, once again. "I'm assuming you'll have a psychiatrist perform a complete analysis on her?" I addressed this to Maxwell.

"Absolutely. She's crazy as a fucking loon. I could give you a copy, if you'd like," he offered. I was suspicious of his generosity but didn't comment on that. Perhaps I misjudged him. Besides, I still wasn't convinced she was crazy, though I had no problem telling her I believed it.

"I'm planning to pitch this story to my boss at the Philly Herald as a piece on female serial killers, and information on the psychology behind it would be very helpful. I will, of course, promise not to use confidential information about Catherine's case in my piece."

"See that you don't, or I'll say you obtained it illegally and sue your asses off."

Okay, perhaps I hadn't misjudged, after all. He was definitely an asshole.

We went over the map of Pennsylvania State for a while. Rather, Shaw and I did, patently ignoring the ferret in the room. Shaw added another bloody circle around the area of Shickshinny. "I'll call over to Luzerne County and have them get started looking for the body of a young man, college age, fitting Catherine's description of him, and cover any missing persons reports from about two years ago. I haven't received any leads yet from Clinton County but hopefully it's just a matter of time before we can corroborate her stories and start building a case. I'm surprised you haven't tried to get her out yet for lack of evidence," Shaw said, looking at Maxwell for the first time in nearly an hour.

"She refuses to speak to me, so I have very little to go on," Maxwell responded, his frustration palpable. "Trust me, I'd be all over you for talking to her yesterday without me present but she insisted. I had to get an injunction from the judge to force my hand."

Shaw and I exchanged a glance. We didn't feel sorry for Maxwell.

It was afternoon already, and while Rick relaxed his deadlines once I started producing--and paying my room and board again--he did get pissy when I sent my daily report after he left the office for the day. "I've got to be running," I announced to the men.

"So do I," Maxwell responded. "I'll walk you out."

"I'll see you both out," Shaw added. Maxwell gave him a cold look but he just smiled blandly.

We headed down the main hall and out the double doors to a bright, sunny afternoon, rare for February in Pennsylvania. I stored my things in the passenger seat of the rental, wrinkling my nose in distaste at the sight of the lawyer's expensive Rolls Royce nudged nearly up my car's tailpipe.

My disgust deepened tenfold when the rodent-like creep oozed his way over to where I stood next to my car and said, "So, Ms. Pascale, how about we go over the tapes from yesterday sometime this evening? I could pick you up around seven and take you back to my place." He actually raised his eyebrows at me, simultaneously licking his lips with a furtive dart of his ferret tongue.

"Actually," Shaw said smoothly, coming to stand close behind me, "Sophia and I already had dinner plans this evening. Maybe some other time, Maxwell." I nodded, grateful for his intervention. I tried to smile at the weasely bastard. I still wanted that psychiatrist's report but not bad enough to spend time alone with that asshole.

"Ok. I see how it is. You two are--a thing? That's kind of a conflict of interest, Shaw," Maxwell snarled. "Best keep that in mind!"

He strode to his car and wrenched open the door, hurled his expensive briefcase into the posh interior and flung himself into the driver's seat. He slammed his door and glared at us, revving the engine before backing up. He put the powerful car in gear and sped down the gravel driveway, spraying rocks everywhere. His tantrum was faintly reminiscent of the murder Catherine just described, and I shivered in the weak winter sun.

I sighed. *There goes the report*, I thought, but honestly it was worth it. I'd come up with something on my own. I turned to Shaw. "Thanks for lying for me."

"Who said anything about lying?"

I gaped at him. Did he just ask me out? "What about the doctor's report? Or the conflict of interest? Can he cause problems for you, because of me?"

"That little fuck? Not a chance. I'll get the warden to have one of his golf buddy judges to demand a copy of that report goes on file with the prison, since we are the only facility in Pennsylvania that can house violent criminals in the entire state and if he's smart, he'll do what he can to get her transferred to a mental institution as soon as possible. I don't think he'll last long enough to do that, though. You heard him--she won't even talk to him. So what do you say? Pick you up at seven, take you to my place, and listen to some murder confessions?" His blue eyes twinkled as he teased me.

"Ha, ha! Very funny. Pick me up at seven is fine though," I added, blushing furiously. I bolted for my car, then remembered he didn't know where I was staying or what my phone number was. I ran back, wrote it down on his hand like a high school girl, and got the hell out of there, cheeks burning with mortification.

I drove at a more sedate pace than Maxwell down the elegantly curved driveway. My elation with the Shaw incident was dampened by the sight of black bird silhouettes outlined in ebony against the blue sky, three now, not two. As I drove under the mantel of stone, I slowed and looked up at them. The smallest one, on the far right, was marked with a splash of white brightening its dark breast. I remembered with a chill the officer on guard had shot one of them, and paid for it with his life.

8-Strength

I prayed for strength, dreading the coming conversation with Rick. Steeling myself, I called him at home, hoping the evening's whiskey had a chance to kick in. He answered on the second ring, sounding mellow. Sweet.

"Hey, there's my girl. How's coal country? Meet any psychos? Not just at the prison," he guffawed at his own lame joke.

"Hi Rick. Just checking in. Brutal day today, let me tell you. If we find evidence that she's telling the truth, this woman is the biggest psychopath anyone has seen in a long time. It's all in my report. I'll send that over to you in a sec. I have a great idea though, and I wanted to run it by you as to my angle on this story."

"Sure, Soph. Fire away."

I told him my idea about doing a series piece on female serial killers. That meant my name in print, associated with a major case, multiple times. I got to the part about obtaining the psychiatrist's report from the lawyer and Rick was ominously silent. Of all the newspaper guys on earth, I thought, I had to apprentice myself to the only one with a mother hen tendency.

"So that's it. That's my idea. What do you think?" I finished.

"Sophia, you're not in over your head out there are you? Not swimming with sharks, right?"

"You have nothing to worry about boss," I said in my most chipper voice, knowing he liked being called boss. "Besides, I'm dating the lead officer, so I couldn't possibly be safer." On that note, I hung up my cell, throwing myself back on the bed and giggling helplessly. I could just imagine the look on his face. Rick, for all that he was a colossal pain in the ass, was also the closest thing I'd had to a father since my parents died. I griped about him a lot to myself, but I worried about disappointing him all the same. I turned my cell on vibrate and got ready for dinner with Shaw. I did my best to calm my nerves. I didn't date much, didn't trust anyone very easily, but I felt safe with Brad. Maybe it was because he already knew my deep secrets, through no fault of my own, my darkness already bared to the light. Or maybe it was the strange, compelling attraction I'd had to him since I'd first laid eyes on him.

I dressed casually in jeans and flowing peasant blouse, unsure what kind of date he had in mind, hoping I wasn't underdressed. I was pacing the floor of my room when a gentle knock startled me so badly I whirled around to answer it and tripped over my own feet. I fell to the floor with a thud and heard Shaw's concerned voice on the other side of the door.

"Sophia? Is that you? Are you okay?"

I popped up like a jack-in-the-box. "Yes! I mean, I'll be right there!" Thank God he didn't have x-ray vision.

I snatched up my purse and hotel key and wrenched open the door. He stood in the hallway, decked out in jeans, boots, a white button-down shirt, and a great fitting tan jacket with patches on the elbows. He had a small bouquet of calla lilies in one hand, thrust toward me like a cross-wielding vampire hunter.

"You look wonderful," he told me. His gaze traveled over me and I blushed like an idiot.

"Thank you! You do too. Here, let me put these in some water."

I left the door open while I ran and grabbed the ice bucket from the bathroom, filling it with water. I put the flowers in the bucket. Their stems were too long for the container and they drooped sadly over the sides. Brad stepped cautiously over the threshold into the room, unsure if he should but apparently determined to help.

"Here, let me."

He pulled the blossoms from the bucket, shook off the excess water, and broke them in half neatly. He plopped them back into the bucket where they arranged themselves beautifully in their makeshift container.

"Thank you," I told him, taking the stem pieces from his hand. Our fingers touched, and that electric shock of static jumped from his skin to mine and back. We were both startled and then laughed nervously. Shaw gestured toward the open door. "Shall we?"

I preceded him and we headed out, with him firmly closing the door behind us. "So, where you taking me, Shaw?"

"Sophia, please. It's Brad. So, what are you up for? Dinner and a movie? Dancing? Skydiving?"

"Pittsburgh is your town...surprise me!"

"You got it!"

He opened his car's passenger door for me. It was a newer model Jeep Cherokee. He whistled cheerfully as he closed my door and hustled over to the driver's side. We smiled at each other as he pulled away from the hotel parking lot, heading west away from town. I was still kind of nervous but I trusted him more with each passing moment, for some reason. Call it intuition, or that something Catherine and my Nonna claimed I had, even blame it on his badge but I had the feeling Brad would never hurt me. I relaxed into my seat, trying to ignore my control freak tendencies and just enjoy the evening.

He turned down a dirt road not far out of town, and began to question my previous assessment of his character. I gave him a pointed look and he removed his gaze from the road long enough to give me a raised eyebrow and half-grin before returning his eyes to the road, navigating the pot holes with an ease that could only be born from practice.

We bumped down a tree-lined lane for a mile or so until we came to a clearing. A rustic log cabin, well maintained, was flanked by a large barn with an adjoining paddock and what looked like miles of pastureland beyond the barn. A wisp of smoke issued from the chimney of the cabin and some distance behind it, a small herd of horses grazed peacefully in the weak afternoon light.

"I hope you don't think this is too forward, but I really did want to bring you to my place. I thought we could ride for a while and then head out to dinner," Brad said, parking the Jeep and looking at me with anxiety written all over his face. "We can totally do something else, though, if this is too much."

I wanted to be mad but was too delighted at the idea of riding. I'd taken an equestrian class in college, which I enjoyed immensely, but otherwise hadn't ridden a horse in years.

"How many horses do you have?" I asked, by way of reassuring him I wasn't mad. He was relieved, and became chatty now that he wasn't going to bear the brunt of my anger.

"Just the four of them. Two mares and two geldings. They're all former trail horses, quarter and thoroughbred mixes. Now they're just my pasture pets most of the time. Since I started on at the prison I haven't spent much time with them."

We got out of the car at the same time, eager to call the horses in. I couldn't wait to meet them. A bundle of black and white fur flew from the barn and sailed over the top spar of the paddock railing, snarling and growling like Cerberus raised from the depths of Hades.

"Brodie! Down!" Brad commanded but the dog paid him little heed. I dropped down to one knee and extended a hand, head bowed and gaze lowered, waiting. The dog ceased raging at me at once and approached on his belly, crouching forward while sniffing my fingers with suspicion.

"I wouldn't..." Brad began but stopped when the

dog whined and rolled on his back, paws waving in the air, presenting his belly to me and making himself vulnerable. I lowered my hand and scratched his exposed stomach, crooning, "Good boy, there's a good sweet boy. Brodie is your name? What a lovely dog you are."

"He bites," Brad finished.

"I'm sure he does."

"He apparently doesn't bite you."

"I have a way with dogs. Always have."

I rose to my feet and Brodie scrambled to his, staring up at me with adoring brown eyes and wagging his tail while he sat. He really was a lovely creature, too, a Border collie was my guess, his black and white coat marked handsomely. Brad shook his head but didn't comment further. He led the way to the barn and I inhaled the nostalgic scent of hay, horses, manure, and tack oil.

Brad grabbed a tin of oats from a large container and rattled it against the bin before filling it. The sound of pounding hoof beats sounded outside, a quick response to the loud banging. We went out the back of the barn to the pasture where the horses waited. A grey, a chestnut, a liver chestnut, and a bay, I recited their colors in my head. I got to know them for a few minutes before choosing the grey, an older mare with a sweet disposition.

We saddled and bridled them, Brad checking my tack before we headed out. I didn't mind, since it had been a while for me. I got the impression he would have checked it no matter what, even if I were a jockey. *A definite overprotective streak*, I thought. *A good quality for a man with his job.*

We mounted and took off, me on the grey and Brad riding the liver chestnut gelding. We headed down the tree lined gravel road we'd driven in on. Brad turned before we reached the main highway, following a trail through the woods that curved around what I assumed was his property.

I sighed in contentment. The woods were so peaceful, hushed, and quiet.

We rode along in silent companionship, enjoying the sights and sounds of the forest, the feel of the horses' powerful bodies beneath us, and the waning light of the day. The sun set quickly in February, and all too soon we were headed back to the barn to brush and wipe down the horses before putting them and their companions in their stalls for the night.

We put the brushes and towels in the tack room. I turned to Brad and said with sincerity, "Thank you for what is possibly the best date I have ever had."

"Possibly? Well it's not over yet so there's still time for me to secure that number one spot."

He put a hand on the door frame above me and leaned in close, watching me carefully before his lips descended upon mine. I sucked in my breath, right palm flat against his chest. In spite of my attraction to him, painful memories started to crowd my mind and I broke free, afraid.

"Easy," he murmured. I started to protest that I wasn't a horse so he didn't need to calm me like one, going on the defensive to cover my embarrassment, but he dropped his other hand to the small of my back and pulled me close against him, kissing me with those soft lips. My body responded, melting into him, while my mind screamed, *Danger!*

I made a small, half-hearted sound of protest that he ignored completely. He kept kissing me, his tongue touching my lips until I finally relented. He wrapped both strong arms around me, deepening his kiss until I squirmed to get away.

"It's okay," he whispered, putting his forehead against mine. He still held me though my breath was coming fast, panic and desire at war within me. We stayed like that for a while, his hands caressing my back and eventually dipping lower, down my ass and back up to caress my neck. It felt amazing, not threatening. I pulled back slightly to look at him.

"I'm sorry, Sophia. I've just wanted to do that for so long..."

"I wanted you to," I whispered. "I'm sorry I'm so scared."

"I'll never push you too far, I promise."

What the hell. As I'd wanted to for a while, I whispered, "I trust you," and gave myself over to him.

His eyes glowed at my words, the worried expression replaced with lust and something like awe. Who knew eyes could look like his? So blue, crackling with electricity. I wanted to drown in them. I'd forgotten Catherine Meara, my boss, Brad's job...even my uncle. All I knew was wanting.

He saw it, my desire for him, and he responded, kissing me again, hands roaming the territory of my body. After a moment, he released me and I felt instantly bereft. He held out a hand and I took it, letting him lead me dreamlike into the cabin. Inside, a fire blazed in the hearth, casting an orange glow on the contents of the room. I wondered if he'd planned this all along, having a fire ready, a pile of quilts on the bed in the corner. Then his lips and hands began weaving their spell on my body again and I forgot to be suspicious. I forgot everything, cleared my mind of all thought and reason, focusing only on feeling every sensation with every nerve ending I possessed.

He undressed me, moving me toward the bed and laying me down to take off my shoes, socks, and jeans. I lay there in my plain white bra and panties, aware of nothing other than the warmth of the fire, the smell of my own longing, and the sight of Brad stripping off his clothes.

His body was strong, muscular, with washboard abs and well-defined arms that were hidden most of the time beneath his clothes. He smiled and lifted me by one hand, unclasping my bra and peeling it slowly down my arms until my full breasts hung free. He laid me back down, pulling my panties off, and sliding them down the length of my legs until I was completely naked before him.

He lay next to me, flipping a quilt over the top of us. I felt him hot and hard against my side and felt a quiver of my old fear returning. "My god, Sophia," he whispered, voice raw with emotion. His mouth claimed me, blazing a trail down from my lips to my throat, then to my breasts, first the right and then the left nipple receiving his tender attention. I arched against him and clenched the blankets in my fists, whimpering at the amazing feelings coursing through my body. My fear was there, right at the surface, held steady by my lust but waiting to pounce. Brad's hands roamed over me, touching me everywhere and rubbing in gentle circular waves. When he decided I was ready, he slid a finger down, inside me. I cried out in pleasure, in fear, my legs parting of their own volition though my mind wished to force them closed.

Brad rose above me on rigid arms, sliding into me with one smooth motion, hearing only pleasure in my sounds. I screamed then, my eyes opening wide, the presence of him nearly too much to bear. My flesh felt as though it would tear, like he would rend me asunder. He held me captive with his gaze, those eyes never moving from mine, willing my fear away. He leaned down, so slowly, and teased my lips again with his own, kissing me over and over until I finally relaxed and began to respond again. My lust came crashing back over me and my hips moved, urging him to do the same. He obliged, very carefully at first, then with increasing intensity. Our bodies were sheened with sweat as we danced against each other, seeking and searching for the crest of the wave.

I cried out again, this time without fear and pain, as my orgasm hit me, barreling through me, and making every muscle and sinew clench at once with its force. Brad watched me, his eyes tracing fire into my flesh as he finished a moment later, burying his head in my shoulder and shuddering with pleasure. We lay like limp rags, breathing hard, for long moments.

"I don't date much," I finally said, "but I have to give you first place now, I think."

Groaning, he pulled out of me with infinite care and rolled to his side. He wrapped his arms around me, spooning me and pulling the quilt back up over our entwined bodies.

"Thank god," he replied. "I don't think I can top that just yet."

I giggled. He sounded so relieved. He propped himself up on an elbow and looked down at me, those amazing eyes mine, all mine.

"You okay?"

"I'll be fine. I am fine. Better than fine." I tried to kiss him but he saw the sheen of tears in my eyes before I could marshal my feelings under control.

"I'm sorry, Sophia," his voice was pained, "you should have stopped me if it was too much..."

"NO! No. I wanted to. I've wanted to since I met you but I let my fear cripple me from pursuing those feelings. It was amazing! Does it always feel like that?"

"Like...what? Did I do something unusual?" He gave a half-laugh.

"I mean...the end part. You know. 'IT.' Does "it" always feel like that?"

"You mean...the orgasm part? You've never had one?" He was incredulous.

I blushed. "No. I told you. I don't date much."

"How much is not much?"

"Um...never?" I made it a question.

"I find it hard to believe a woman as beautiful, intelligent, and talented as you has never dated."

"I've had 'dates' but I never let it go far."

"So you've never had...sex?"

"Not willingly, no. Well, I mean. I have now."

He said nothing, just turned the full power of that intense gaze on me. Finally, he gathered me close and held me for a long time, until I slipped into the first dreamless sleep I'd had since coming here. We awoke three more times in the night, making love and raiding his fridge, talking until the sun came up. We showered together, joints creaky with overuse. We played and laughed with each other while doing his morning's chores, feeding horses and Brodie. We kept sneaking in long kisses, making the morning rounds take twice as long, he claimed.

Finally, with great reluctance, he drove me back to my hotel. He parked, coming up to my room with me and saying he couldn't bear to be parted with me for a single instant. It was corny, but so romantic I played along.

We made love in my hotel bed of course. We were like two teenagers who couldn't get enough of each other. Now that the dam of fear inside me was broken, I wanted to climb into bed with him forever and shut the world away. We had to shower again, this time quickly. I dressed and grabbed my things. At my car, he kissed me so thoroughly my toes curled. "Ah, hell," he sighed. "Real life is intruding on my dream come true."

"Come on, my own personal Romeo. I'll race you to the prison."

"You'll do no such thing or I'll be forced to arrest you for disorderly conduct, driving while intoxicated and/or sleep deprived, and a host of other things that will keep you in Pittsburgh for the foreseeable future."

"Well I could think of worse fates." I stuck out my tongue at him and he swatted me on the ass. I got into my car and he raced for his, ending the best date of my entire life.

****

Catherine, of course, knew instantly. "Well, well. How coarse and cliché, Sophia. Rutting like an animal with our Officer Shaw? What would your grandmother say?"

"She'd probably say "good for me," Catherine. You should get laid now and then, it does wonders for the tension." If she was going to bait me, then turnabout was fair play.

"Don't pretend with me Sophia. Tell me, how often did your uncle's face intrude on your fuckfest with Dudley Do Right? Or was he not that great, our Officer Shaw? Did you welcome your uncle's presence in bed with you, out of boredom?"

I mentally counted to ten, calming myself down and hoping my anger wouldn't show. I fervently prayed Brad didn't believe what she was saying. Yes, I'd been afraid, but hopefully he knew I'd gotten over it, thanks to him. I returned my thoughts to the dangerous viper sitting shackled at the table. "Now who's slumming, Catherine? Prying details of my sex life because you can't have one of your own?"

"Oh, have I upset you Sophia?"

"Not at all. I'm just waiting for you to get around to it, rather than focusing rather immaturely on matters which do not pertain to our purpose here."

She tried to cross her arms but the handcuffs prevented it. She settled on clenching her hands together tightly, bloodless knuckles pressed against one another like marbles beneath her skin. "Fine. The next card was Strength. I'd ditched the beautiful boy's car somewhere north of Williamsport and hitched into town. As usual, I managed to find a job as a waitress in an Italian restaurant downtown. Before too long, the dark lord was whispering his sweet nothings into my ear.

"We chose a woman this time, a lone girl a few years younger than me. She looked kind of like me, with red hair, slightly paler skin and only blue eyes, not special eyes." This was said with a glance in Brad's direction, intended to insult him and his 'only' blue eyes. "She was alone every time she came into my restaurant and the dark lord took a fancy to her. She was pathetically stupid though, but a perfect mark. She had no one in the world to care for her, she said. Both of her parents were dead, just like yours and mine, and she had no kin. We were two orphans in the world. She clung to me like a barnacle and I patiently waited for the manner in which Strength was to manifest itself. I wanted to prove myself, to move one step closer to His loving embrace. Waiting was delicious too, but difficult, like a long-awaited meal or the yearning for ice cream. Satisfied at last.

"I taught her, you know. I taught her most everything. How to cast a circle. How to perform the blood ritual, what the symbols meant. She was so dumb, so fucking stupid, I had difficulty keeping my temper. Sometimes I would beat her, with my fists or a belt, but never left a mark. She lived in this halfway house and it wouldn't do for anyone to find out about our friendship. Not that anyone would believe a retard like her anyway. She would crawl to me, after I lost my temper and beat her, begging and crying, dripping snot everywhere. Begging me to forgive her. The stupid cow. I prayed to the Horned God to show me the way, to help me gain the Strength that was required. Finally, my prayers were answered.

"I lured her to an empty warehouse by promising to teach her the sacrificial ritual, the one thing I had yet to show her. She thought she was going to learn how to make an offering and impress the dark lord but instead she was the sacrifice. I tricked her, telling her to draw the raven across her breasts in her own blood and she did. I'd made her bring a live chicken, telling her she was to sacrifice it.

"I told her to kneel in front of the altar and lean over to cut the bird's head off so it wouldn't spray the altar cloth.

The fucking moron! How many times had I told her about the symbols, about the raven? How many times had I told her, over and over again, that you have to cast the fucking circle first, before any ritual?" Catherine's voice had been flat and neutral, like she was reciting a grocery list. Now her pitch heightened, her anger making her loud and shrill, her face contorted with the force of her rage.

"She deserved it! As if she would ever be as powerful as me. Her, a stupid cow, a fucking retard, chewing her cud! An idiot who couldn't remember the simplest directions! She raised the machete I brought, way over her head, and slashed it down on the chicken's neck, screaming in her stupid retard voice the whole time. But I shut her up good, didn't I? Yes. I sure did. That chicken wasn't the only thing that lost its head.

"I'd already cast my circle, you see. Of course. Because I'm not an idiot. With every ounce of strength in my body, I sliced her head off as she sat there hunched and crying over the limp body of the chicken she'd decapitated. Her head rolled off much cleaner than the head of the chicken. I hacked her body to pieces. My arms hurt so badly the next day I could barely lift them, but it was worth it. I arranged her pieces around the altar and drew the raven on the altar cloth with my blood as required, since there weren't very large pieces of her left to draw on. I left her and got the hell out of there. It was an abandoned warehouse in a crappy part of town but you never know when some nosy cop might come around and interrupt one's freedom of religion."

She finished with a gloating expression planted on her pretty face, giving Brad a nasty smile before turning her attention back to me. "You go fuck your nosy cop, Sophia. Then come back and we'll play show and tell."

I gave her a cold look but said nothing, hauling my briefcase with the rolling voice recorder, taking my anger, fear, and frustration with me.

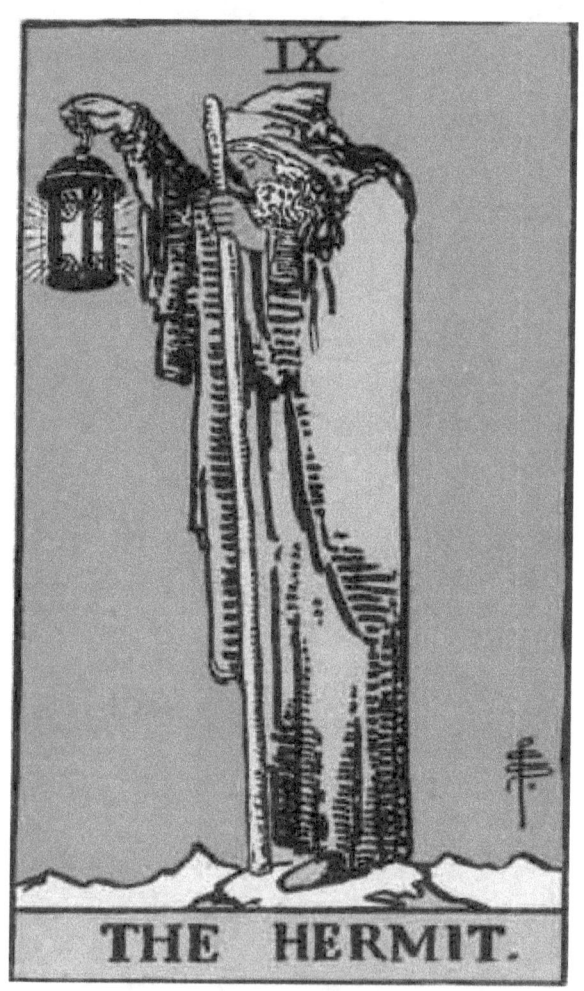

9-The Hermit

I followed Brad, as usual to his office. We made it inside the door before collapsing in each other's arms.

"I don't know about you, but these stories of hers are getting harder and harder for me to hear," I said, my voice muffled against his shoulder.

"I've only been here a few months but I was a beat cop and then a detective for a long time. You never get used to hearing this shit, not ever." His voice floated above my head. "You're doing a great job of getting her to talk. We need her to give us names but don't tell her personal information about yourself. She's a fucking monster. You don't want her in your head."

I nodded. After long moments we broke apart, comforted by the contact and ready to keep working. We sat together in the leather seats, Brad circling Catherine's latest supposed crime scene with the red circle. "How's the investigation going so far with what she's given us?" I asked.

"My Clinton County contact is Dayne Yoakum, one of those good old boys. Probably sleeps in his cowboy boots. He's running missing persons and coordinating a search, since Sunbury rolled the dice and got rid of her to us. It's nice to have the extra help. Plus, Yoakum offered to work up surrounding counties, said he has contacts within those other departments. Guess I shouldn't complain about how long it's taking but dammit, I'm losing patience. What if she decides to stop talking?"

"I thought you told Maxwell you hadn't heard from anyone in Clinton County?"

He grinned. "Yeah, that's what I told him all right."

"You're bad. I worry about her stopping, too, though. Part of me wishes she would stop, that there was no more for her to say, but at the same time, this story could make my career."

"Then you'd leave, right? If the story was over?"

His tone was teasing but there was an undercurrent there. I remembered suddenly, for no reason, I'd only packed for a week's stay. A week? A lifetime? What was he asking?

"Well, maybe not right away," I hedged. He smiled, white teeth flashing briefly in his handsome face before he kissed me softly.

"I have to go write up my nightly report for my boss, regretfully," I said when the kiss ended.

"Would you be adverse to a little Chinese take-out and Irish guy at your hotel later?"

Now it was my turn to grin at him. "Only if you bring your handcuffs," I teased.

"Oh, really? Have I created a monster?"

"I never said the handcuffs were for me."

You can guess how that conversation ended.

The gate guards nodded to me as I left, and one actually smiled. My buoyant mood was crushed by the sight of a fourth raven perched on the upper pediment, beady black eyes staring down at me through the windshield.

****

I woke the next morning, tangled in the blankets, terror shrieking through my veins. Shreds of my nightmare played behind my eyes and the sound of beating wings echoed in my ears. Gradually the sound was replaced by the water pouring in the shower. Brad must be in there, I thought. Suddenly, I didn't want to be alone anymore with Catherine's ghosts.

I padded naked into the hotel bathroom and pulled open the shower curtain. After we certainly cost the hotel a pretty penny in hot water usage, we dressed and grabbed a coffee and breakfast at a diner Brad was familiar with. They made a pretty decent omelet, which I ate while I pondered our burgeoning relationship. He'd brought clothes, more than one set, and a toothbrush. What did that mean?

We headed to the prison in my rental. Brad had a few things to take care of at his office, and I was early for my appointment with Catherine. I was somewhat surprised I hadn't seen the lawyer again. Maybe he was as freaked out by her as everyone else, including me. Plus, we didn't really have anything to charge her with, though the lawyer was supposed to protect her from herself. No evidence had been found that she was even telling the truth, though, and eventually, if something didn't come to light soon, Catherine Meara would be set free upon an unsuspecting world again.

I braced myself for more acerbic comments from her about the subject of my sex life but as usual her mood was unpredictable. The snappy, bitchy mood from yesterday was replaced with the melancholy unhappiness she'd displayed when talking about her "pretty boy."

"My next raven was chosen by my dark lord and the Hermit card. I'd hitched as far as I could from where I'd killed the stupid girl but I got lost. I wandered for days in the woods, so thirsty and hungry. Can you imagine it? All these things I'd done, all I'd lived through, only to be lost in the forest. I felt forsaken, I felt the Goddess's hand all around me, and her hatred of me. I was alone and cold and afraid, again. Have you ever woken to find yourself living in a nightmare? That's what it was like. I wondered if the dark lord had forsaken me, but then on the magic day, the seventeenth day, I found the shack in the clearing, surrounded by smaller buildings. I'd survived on berries and leaves, and rain when it rained or dew from the trees when it didn't. The shack was like a beacon of hope, a symbol of civilization, no matter how pathetic it seemed.

"Smoke curled from the crumbling chimney. I was so cold, I wanted to rush to its source and bury myself in it. I haven't lived this long, or done the things I've done, by letting misery cloud my judgment. I crept around the back of the building to a sagging window, looking inside for the source of the fire. There was an old man sitting there in a rocking chair next to a potbellied stove, covered with a quilt. He was reading a book, just rocking back and forth. It was late October, I think, by this time and cold as hell in those mountains. I shivered more at the sight of such warmth, a luxury I'd not known for a long time.

"I made myself retreat to the woods, begging my dark lord to let me sacrifice the man and steal his fire. After many hours of hoping and praying, I finally heard His blessed voice whisper on the wind, sighing through the leaves of the trees with a sibilant whisper. He approved my choice and I was ecstatic once more, no longer feeling the cold, bathed in the glow of His love.

"I waited until the old man's light went out. Since there were no power lines to cut I assumed he used kerosene lanterns for lighting. It was very rustic, suitable for a hermit. I snuck into his house while he slept. He didn't even lock his door. I was quiet and careful but it wouldn't have mattered. He slept like an old tired man, snoring too loud to hear anything and sure he was safe in his own bed in the middle of nowhere.

"I'd found a rope in one of the outbuildings and brought it in with me. He had an indoor garden in one of those littler shacks and I gorged myself earlier on hothouse tomatoes and strawberries. Another of the smaller buildings was clearly where he butchered meat, deer or such, since there were wicked looking meat hooks hanging from the ceiling and blood stains on the dirt floor. That room looked interesting but the dark lord whispered that it was not to be. I moved on.

"Even better was the building which housed an old truck. It was pretty well maintained; it looked shiny, polished, and well cared for. I couldn't tell you the make or year, but it was pretty old, maybe even a classic. I didn't care what it was as long as it had four wheels and rolled me away from there.

"The rope was in a building that served as sort of a shop. There were tools of all kinds stored in there, and objects made of wood. I stole the rope and while he slept, I tied the old man to the bed. He never stirred as I wrapped the rope around his body and the bed frame, over and over, until he was like a fly in a spider's web. In a way, I guess he was."

"Catherine, do you have the names of any of these people? What was the old man's name?" I was hoping she would give me something for Brad to go on, remembering our conversation the day before.

"I don't know the old man's name. I never bothered to find out. My beautiful boy's name was Jason. The stupid girl was Melissa. There are a few more whose names I do know, but each in their turn, Sophia."

"That's fair enough, I guess. What happened to the old man?"

"He drew the Hermit card, as I've said."

"Can you tell me more about what that means?"

"It means he lived and died right there in that little shack, like the hermit he was. It took him much longer to die than I thought it would, but finally he went. As always, I performed the ritual in blood. Then I left and took the old guy's truck to Renovo. The dark lord said the next raven was waiting there, just south a ways. I dumped the truck in town, cleaned it of prints and signs of me, and let my feet take me where I was needed next."

"What do you mean, "It took him longer to die than you thought?""

"Well, I always read that it takes the human body something like three days maximum to die of dehydration but he lasted almost two weeks strapped to that bed."

"You...you left him there, tied up? And watched him die?" I felt as though I might throw up.

She seemed genuinely puzzled by my distress. "Yeah, sure. I mean, that was his fate. He had to die as he'd lived, that was the meaning of the Hermit card."   I   was stunned. I'd heard her spout descriptions of brutal murders for several days now but somehow this was worse. It was more real. I needed to be sick.

"Would you excuse me for a moment?"

"Sure. Go have a quickie with our Officer Shaw," she said with disinterest. She laid her head on the wooden table as I left.

I ran out of her cell and down the hallway to the bathroom near the officer's hub. I went into a stall and threw up my omelet and coffee from the morning. I rinsed my mouth and splashed some water on my face. Brad was waiting for me outside the bathroom. He gave me a brief hug and then said, "Can you keep going?"

I sensed some excitement. "Why? What happened?"

"One of my officers took my place for a few minutes. You didn't notice and I don't blame you. Yoakum called to say they have a missing person's case out of Luzerne County for a young man matching Catherine's description of the boy she ran over with his car. Name of Jason White, age twenty-two, missing since August 2011. His car was a 2000 Honda Accord, dark maroon, never recovered."

"Oh, my God. Brad, she just told me his name was Jason. She said the girl's name was Melissa, and she didn't know the names of the two lovers in the woods or the old man she tied to the bed but that there were more she did know."

"Luzerne County Sherriff's office is out combing

the woods to find White's body. And get this, Melissa Anselme, age nineteen, went missing from the halfway house she was staying at in November 2011, two months after Catherine claims she killed White. She was reported missing in Lycoming County fairly quickly since she was mildly mentally retarded. The halfway house freaked out when she didn't come home from her part time job that day. She fits Catherine's physical description as well. I came back in time to hear her confirm the second victim's name to you."

I forced my revulsion aside. "I can stay as long as necessary. If she will only talk to me, we'll stay here all night if we have to. I'll try to get more names and locations from her."

"You're doing great. Meantime, I'll get back with Yoakum, see if any old guys living in the woods have come up on his radar. I doubt it. There are places in the Appalachians where you can just disappear and no one would ever know. I'm also going to call her weasel lawyer and see when he can get that psychiatrist in here. I'd like to have this bitch transferred out of my prison as soon as possible."

I nodded. I wanted nothing more than to leave with him and let us lose ourselves in one another but we both had jobs to do. These feelings for Brad were all new, and I was unsure what they meant, exactly. Focusing on the job at hand helped push the doubts and fears away. Pulling information from her was no longer exciting but the idea of a Pulitzer started circling around my subconscious. Brad left, ensuring another officer was to stand guard at the door.

I went back to where she sat with her head on the table, chained like a beast. I hoped they'd burn her at the stake like a real witch. I quickly put aside the thought the same fate could be had for me, too.

Catherine raised her head and smiled, another facet of her ever-changing personality coming to the forefront.

No doubt she's gleaned what I was thinking. I forged on, wary of who and what I was dealing with.

"Sorry about that. You were saying?"

"Did they find the bodies yet, Sophia?"

"No, nothing to corroborate your stories so far, Catherine. Will there be?"

"You sound so disappointed. I would think a fainting flower, bleeding heart type such as yourself would be glad the corpses weren't piling up. Then you could tell yourself the wicked witch isn't real. Then again, neither would you be."

"I hope this is an elaborate hoax, Catherine. That's still a hell of a story for me, either way."

"Nice try. Really, bravo. Sounding all cold-blooded and shit. Good for you." Sarcasm dripped from her words like poison.

"Let's stop the bullshit now and focus on why we're here, once again."

"You have no idea why you're here, Sophia, so shut the fuck up and let me say whatever I want."

"Fine, that's fine. Go right ahead."

She leaned forward, chains rattling like a ghost. "You will be tested at the end, bitch. Remember that."

I just stared at her, waiting. Finally, she started speaking again.

10-Wheel of Fortune

"I dumped the old guy's truck in Renovo, like I said," Catherine's musical voice echoed around the cell's concrete walls.

"They have slot machines at the Green Lantern in Renovo, did you know that?"

"I didn't but it fits the Wheel of Fortune card nicely," I replied, striving for a matter-of-fact tone.

Anticipating her next card didn't endear me to her. "Clever. Yes it does have that synchronicity that I find comforting. I worked there, at the Green Lantern, where I met the next raven. He was a regular, feeding coin after coin into the machines. A weird older guy, wore thick glasses and wouldn't talk to anyone. Except me, of course," she smirked.

"Of course."

Her mood was suddenly buoyant, somewhat nostalgic. "His name was Finneaus Parsons. I remember it because he went by Finn, which is a strange name but kind of cool. He told me the whole thing like he was proud of it. Always ordered a glass of milk and a turkey sandwich. He was extremely particular too, drove the other waitresses and the cook nuts but it didn't bother me. He would only drink two percent milk in a frost chilled mug and he had to have his sandwich delivered all deconstructed, the pieces put on a plate so he could sniff them before he put the sandwich together himself."

"Sounds like he had some control issues. Odd for a gambler."

"I thought so too. Great minds think alike, eh Sophia?" She winked at me. "Anyway, Finn was nice to me, always tipped exactly fifteen percent. I was a little sad when the dark lord said he was the sacrifice but honestly it sort of seemed like a mercy, like I was doing him a favor.

"I told him I was taking classes online so I could get out of waitressing. He was impressed by that, always offering his help. Finn was super smart, like one of those geniuses you hear about on TV. One day, I took him up on his offer and asked if I could stop by after my shift. He did me one better and offered to drive me to his house where we could use his computer, rather than me having to type it up at the library. Then he said he'd drive me home afterward. 'Home' was a shabby motel in a bad part of town but he didn't need to know that. I agreed but only after he agreed it was nothing sexual. It was like he got off on the idea of helping me better myself; that was his high. I'm not even sure he liked women."

"So you killed this man, this Finn Parsons, because you thought he was gay?" I fished for details.

"Don't be stupid Sophia. I don't give a shit where men stick it as long as it's not in me. The dark lord commanded and I obeyed."

"Okay, so you killed him because your imaginary husband told you to…" I goaded.

Her eyes flashed with anger but she smiled. "However you want to say it, the man is still dead by my hand as tribute to my one true god. His death served not only its intended purpose but was also a lot of fun for me."

"Fun? How so?"

"Well I told you he was real smart right? He thought I needed help with a history class and was pretty chatty about it. He told me about this thing that Mongol executioners used to do to their victims. They'd take each body part and write it down on three pieces of paper and put it in a basket. The executioner--who was called the Tickler, isn't that awesome?--would pull a piece of paper out of the basket. Then he would 'tickle' the body part listed on the paper. So a foot, for example, would get the attention. But he couldn't just cut it off, see? Because what if he drew that part again? So he might break it the first time, burn it the second time, and *then* cut it off if he got it the third time."

"Dear god..." I choked. "Did you...do this...to him?"

"Of course! After he told me about it, I had to try it. He practically fed me his own death. After we got to his place, I excused myself to go to the bathroom. When I came out, I hit him over the head with the toilet back while he was typing at his computer. His back was turned to the hallway where I came from and he never saw it coming.

"He was pretty tall and heavy, so I rummaged in his kitchen until I found some duct tape. I taped him to the computer chair so I wouldn't have to move him, since he was just slumped forward onto the desk anyway when I smacked him with the heavy toilet lid. I grabbed some plain white paper from his printer and tore it into little strips so I could make the papers with the body parts while I waited for him to wake up. I found some yellow sticky notes and colored pencils so I made use of those while I was at it. It took him a long time to wake up. I started to worry I'd killed him until I realized I could see his chest move up and down while he breathed. So I used my time wisely and gathered some tools from his garage. He didn't have much. He was mostly into computers I guessed but I found a few things. I also found a safe under the bed with a wad of cash in it, about twenty thousand dollars. I figured I'd make it look like arson with robbery when I was done. I had to remind myself not to cut off any parts. A charred body wouldn't be hacked up if it was simple robbery as the motive.

When he woke up we had some fun. There was an electric drill, some sandpaper, a small torch--no idea why he had that but it was really useful..."

"No more," I whispered. "I get the idea."

"You didn't even ask about the four parts that are instantly fatal," Catherine replied. She sounded like a disappointed child, petulant and whiny.

"I don't need to know."

"You were the one who knew what card it was, you know everything, right Sophia? Besides, you need to know how he died silly. See, those Mongols were hard asses but fair. Each of the four fatal parts of the body--the heart, lungs, stomach and brain--were put in the basket four times too. If one of those got pulled, then it was game over for the poor bastard who was the Tickler's meat of the moment."

I hoped I wouldn't puke again in so many minutes. My mouth still tasted sour from the last time. "You drew one of these papers, then?" I guessed.

"Oh yeah, but not for hours and hours!" she said, gleeful. "I wrote those on the yellow sticky notes."

"Christ."

She winked conspiratorially at me, like we two girls shared a secret. "Nope, not him."

I cleared my throat. It took a couple of tries. "What did you do…after?"

"After," she mimicked, "I peeled off the duct tape and laid him out on the floor before his blood cooled and settled. Then I trashed the place and stole all his money, took anything of value I could find. Damn, that was fun too. All the smashing and breaking.

"Then I wiped off all the things I'd touched. I knew that my hair and skin were there, all over, but I figured the fire would take care of that. I used a couple bottles of starter fluid he had stored next to the barbeque as an accelerant and I torched his house. I took his car before it started really well, unfortunately, but I had to go before anyone saw smoke. I finally ditched that piece of shit car in a swamp near Sugarcreek."

"What kind of car was it?"

"One of those little mini car things, looks like a go cart. I don't know what they're called. Damn thing rattled the whole way from his place."

"So you didn't do the circle, the raven's blood offering, or any of your rituals for this victim?"

"Of course I did. I figured you were getting tired of hearing about all that since you stubbornly cling to your 'God' and 'Christ'," she mocked.

"I was just curious if you were having a crisis of faith."

"A crisis of faith? These are words for the weak-minded, Sophia, for losers like that fallen Catholic Irish cop you are now so in love with."

I blushed. I was recording this for Brad to listen to, and because I always recorded these conversations. *He will hear that*, I thought, *but what will he make of it?* Merely Catherine's taunting or the truth as it was beginning to dawn on me?

"Ooh that's a nice shade of red, Sophia," she taunted, overly loud, like a mean kid in a schoolyard. As usual with Catherine, the unexpected was the norm.

"So what happened when you got to Sugarcreek?" I was proud of my steady voice.

"The same thing that always happens. I killed someone."

11-Justice

She sat still with her hands clasped in front of her like an obedient child, yet another of her many facets swimming to the surface of her strange eyes like sharks to a pool of blood.

"The next two ravens fell together though I hadn't yet drawn a card since I killed the history guy. It was just a lucky day I guess. I was in the act of ditching history guy's car in a woodsy area outside Sugarcreek when I heard gunshots. It freaked me out for a minute because I thought it was directed at me. I ran from the car quick and hid in a clump of bushes, but after a few minutes I figured out the shots were coming from farther away than I thought, echoing through the trees.

"I was curious, and heard the welcome sound of the dark lord's urging in the wind, so I crept through the trees until I found this huge black truck, you know the kind, with huge tires?"

I nodded.

"So, anyway," she continued, "the passenger door was wide open so I peeked inside. There was all kinds of shit in there but the best thing was the crossbow on the passenger's seat and the pistol in the center console.

"I stole them both, tucking the gun in the waistband of my jeans so I didn't drop it. I've never handled a crossbow before but it felt right, somehow, in my hands. Honestly, Sophia, I felt like a badass with all those weapons hanging off me. I took the keys out of the ignition and stuck them in my pocket. I decided to hide close by the truck so that when whoever owned it came back, I could sacrifice them to the dark lord as like a bonus, then steal their truck and their gear. Though I hadn't drawn a card yet, I felt confident I was doing His bidding. I snuck away from the giant truck, but right away I knew I had to change course because as soon as I stepped into the cover of the trees, I saw the bodies."

"Bodies? There were other killers in the woods besides you?" I interjected.

"Depends on your point of view, I guess. Depends on your 'religion'," she replied, giving me a sly look from the bottoms of her eyes. "There were animals strewn all over the forest floor. Every few hundred yards, the body of a dead animal lay empty in the gloomy mist. It was January, and the bodies were stiff so it was hard to tell how long they'd lain there. Most of them were varmints, possums and raccoons. One big lump turned out to be a deer but there were numerous birds lying in feathery heaps. It was a massacre. The hunters must have lured the animals there to slaughter them. I didn't know what their reason was, meat or furs or sport, but I didn't want them to come back and find me so I decided to hide in the bed of the truck until whoever was killing all the animals came back."

"You hid in the truck? Weren't you afraid they'd see you and kill you?"

"No. They were stupid. Once I got into the truck bed, I could hear them calling to each other. They were so loud it was a wonder any animals within a hundred miles came near them. I never found out how they'd managed to kill all those creatures but the dark lord was livid and I waited eagerly to make it right."

"You knew there was more than one because you heard them talking?"

"Once the shooting stopped, I could hear them shouting to each other. Two men, by the sound and number of their voices. I lay in the bed of the truck on my stomach with the gun in my left hand, safety off and rounds checked. I didn't know much about guns, but hey, I watch television. I knew to make sure the damned thing would work when I needed it to. I loved that crossbow but knew it would be a detriment when facing armed hunters. I had the element of surprise but if they were both carrying shotguns and rifles, the crossbow would be too slow. So I waited, listening to them kill everything they could find besides each other before they got tired and headed back to the truck.

"They were so loud! Laughing and high-fiving each other, bragging about their kills. They didn't scare me. I leapt up from the bed of the truck before they could notice the missing weapons from inside the truck. Two men, an old guy with white hair and a younger guy with a baseball hat on were less than three feet from the truck. Both carrying a gun in one hand and the dead body of a pheasant in the other. I shot the young guy in the chest, the recoil from the pistol nearly spinning me around. I saw the young guy go down in a splash of neon orange and crimson blood. The old guy stood there in shock with his mouth gaping open. He looked like a fish gasping for air. I crouched down quickly in case he came to his senses, making a smaller target of myself, and fired a round into his face. The bullet went wide and a little too low. I got him in the throat and he died on his feet in a spray of blood, gore cascading down the front of him in a sheet. He fell over at the end, face first in the frozen ground.

"The second recoil knocked me on my ass so I just sat there for a minute and thanked the Horned God for beginner's luck. After a few moments, the birds started singing again and the forest came back to life. I took it as a sign of approval. I pulled my cards out of my back pocket and found the Justice Card face up instead of face down like the rest of the cards in the deck. I guess I'd drawn the next card, after all." Catherine gave me that sly look again, as though she'd fooled me somehow.

"Those two dudes were really heavy, but I dragged them to a spot in the middle of the dirt track they'd parked their truck on and cast the circle. The ravens watched me open their shirts and draw their symbol on the dead flesh with my living blood. I swear, they looked proud of my prowess. I had some fun for a while after the ritual was complete, shooting the crossbow bolts into their bodies until they looked like porcupines. I left the crossbow, sadly, and all their other things with them. I kept the pistol and took the truck. I figured they didn't need it anymore," she laughed.

"Did you know the names of these hunters?"

"Nope. The truck didn't have any papers in it or anything. I looked because I was curious to see if I could tell anything about them by their name or birthday if I could find it."

"Why is that? What would you be able to tell by that information?"

She grew irritated, scowling at me with her perfect face. "Don't play stupid, Sophia, you know what power lies within a name and a day. If I could figure that out, maybe I could figure out how they lured those animals in. That's useful information for a witch."

"You mean...the numbers right?" I was casting my mind back to the occult article for information about names and birthdates. I remembered something about the significance of numerology for many pagan and Wiccan religions. Catherine studied me a moment and then her brow smoothed. She launched into a diatribe, using a somewhat pedantic tone, like a teacher lecturing her class.

"That's right. Names translate to numbers, and birthdates have powerful numbers of their own. As I'm sure you can guess, my name number and my birth number match. Do I have to tell you how uncommon that is?"

"Is it uncommon?"

"It's nearly unheard of. I've never met anyone else who has numbers that align, until I saw your story and byline in the paper. I did some research on you after reading your article. I sort of remembered you, like I said, but after that I was curious. Guess what I found out? You are just like me, whether you like it or not. Both of us have matching name and birth numbers and what's more, it's the same number."

"Seventeen," I whispered.

"Exactly!" Her voice echoed her delight, bouncing around the room to crash against me. "Seventeen, Sophia. It's the month in the Egyptian calendar when Osiris was killed. It's the number of chapters in the Persian bible. And it's the birth and name number of us both. Do you know the significance of that number for you and me?"

I shook my head, unable to speak. I was gripped with an unreasonable dread that we should share anything that was supposedly that powerful.

"A person who has the seventeen birth or name number is considered an incredibly gifted psychic. Or witch, to use outdated vernacular. We have the ability to achieve immortality, Sophia," her voice took on a fanatic, urgent edge. "Think about it! Our names could live on forever. The two of us together are more powerful than any force the rest of simple-minded humanity could ever dream of. I knew from high school you would never join your power with mine. You always kept your distance from me and my kind. You've spent your whole life denying what you are, that's always been plain. Just because you deny its existence doesn't mean it stops existing, Sophia, and so I decided to use it against you. You will be my ticket to immortality and I will leave you in my dust!"

She finished her speech and sat back with her usual self-satisfied expression. I rose to my feet, done listening to her for one day, for a lifetime, I wished. "I was wrong about you. You're batshit crazy," I told her, and walked out.

****

Brad was on the phone when I tapped on his office door and let myself in, not waiting for a response. His shirt sleeves were rolled up, muscular forearms exposed. His hair looked as though he'd run his hands through it repeatedly, his tie was missing, and he wore an expression of extreme frustration. I felt it safe to assume that his day had sucked as badly as mine.

"I don't give a fuck what he's got scheduled this week, you get him here tomorrow, you weasel faced little prick!" he finally yelled into the phone and snapped it shut, tossing it on the desk with not quite enough force to break it.

"That goddamn asshole Maxwell says he'll get the psychiatrist in here sometime next week! I want that fucking bitch out of my prison a hell of a lot sooner than that. Last night she lured another one of my officers into her cell and offered him sex. The dumbass believed her and she bit a hunk of flesh out of the side of his neck and almost killed him. Then while he was screaming and bleeding she sat there finger painting with his blood while humming a fucking lullaby!"

"What? She didn't say anything about it to me during our talk today!"

"It's on the goddamn night surveillance video! I just found out about it myself. I've had call after call from the warden wanting to know why I didn't come down here last night and why he had to instead. All my officers are reporting to him that she's mind fucking them, I've got shit going down in the middle of the night no one is reporting to me because, I quote, 'We thought you were busy with that reporter,' end quote. To top it off, Yoakum has come up with a total of zero bodies in four counties and the state cannot prosecute without any evidence aside from her supposed testimony. And yet I have done nothing about any of it because of my obsession with you! What a fucking mess!" He was shouting by the end of all this, glaring at me with stormy blue eyes.

I was hurt beyond belief but I held my ground. Chin lifted defiantly, I pointed out that none of the problems he was facing were my fault. We stared at each other for a minute, then I admitted defeat. I took the voice recorder from my jacket pocket and placed it gently on the corner of his desk. I gathered the rest of my things from the leather chair and left, closing the door behind me. I was nearly to the front doors when I heard the glass in other office doors shatter in my wake, but I kept going. I didn't start crying until I passed through the double gates, barely registering the now eight black shapes perched solemnly above.

12-The Hanged Man

I'd gotten myself sort of under control by the time I reached my hotel. I was even grimly happy for a few moments that Brad's Jeep was stuck in the hotel parking lot with him miles away at the prison. Then, I was sad again. What kind of vindictive person was I? Was this what love does to people? I'd be alone forever with that kind of thinking.

I must have looked pretty awful because the front desk clerk took one look at me and said, "Oh honey, are you okay?"

I gave her a tremulous smile and nodded, not trusting myself to speak. Whenever I was upset, the kindness of others seemed only to serve as an illuminated back drop to my misery, making everything seem worse. I climbed onto the elevator and rode to my second floor room, leaking a little from the eyes. I had to get a grip. It wasn't like Brad was my husband, or even really a boyfriend, I reminded myself. People had flings all the time. That's all it was.

In my room, I soaked in a blistering hot tub for a few minutes and then dressed in comfy pj's. Still sad but in control of the water works, I researched the psychoses of serial killers before composing my segment for Rick. Though it was later than I usually returned after a session with Catherine, I had plenty of time before deadline and was able to correlate some information I found with what Catherine was claiming she'd done. Her nomadic behavior, and the indigent nature of her chosen profession was in keeping with serial killer profiling. Though most serial killers were male, female serial killers were not completely unheard of. Catherine, however, was sort of unique in some ways. She killed in a variety of ways, though recorded female serial killer activity typically involved poison or guns, less close up work with knives or other stabbing type weapons. According to Catherine, she'd killed with knives as well as other instruments that ensured she would have to do close up work, making the killing more personal.

I had no way of knowing whether she tortured animals when she was younger but my hunch said no, in spite of data to the contrary regarding serial killer behavior and progression. Her reaction to the killing of the animals in the forest by the two hunters would indicate her religious nature, and reverence for flora and fauna, prohibited the torture of lower creatures.

She did fit the profile in many other ways though. Her victims, so far, were all white, as she was. I'd wait to include this in my write ups until her complete victim list was available and confirmed. She was disorganized, choosing victims seemingly at random as well as disorganization in the nature and location of the murders. I resolved to keep a map of my own, pinpointing the locations of her supposed kills and checking for possible patterns.

Catherine's parents were both dead and she'd been raised by grandparents, another commonality among serial killers. Then again, so had I, and I wasn't a murderer. I made a note to check out the grandparents to see if I could match information on her childhood with a typical psychopathic profile.

She fit in the serial killer profile very well with her timeframe and schedule, however. According to my calculations based on information she'd provided so far, her cycle was about every forty-two days between murders. I wondered if her kill cycle matched her menstrual cycle, if her menstruation was off somehow, irregular, if this might cause some of these behaviors on a chemical level. I made another note to find a doctor who could answer questions about it.

Finally, Catherine was very clever and seemed articulate but not especially smart. I didn't believe we were dealing with a genius psychopath but rather one who may be slightly below average intelligence. Sometimes her speech pattern revealed a facet of this, though she strove to cover it with a contrived air of intelligence. It was like a persona that she wore, one that slipped every now and then to reveal the true face hiding beneath the surface.

I compiled some information for further use and composed my piece for the paper, glad I now had a good handle on the psychological side in spite of the lack of a profile on Catherine herself. I decided to shy away from the religious angle in my piece, which is why I sold the female serial killer thing to Rick in the first place. I felt uncomfortable blaming witchcraft because I felt as though the public would read Satanism instead. For some reason, the idea bothered me.

Rick called as soon as I sent the piece over. "Great job, Soph, really good stuff. How's it going over there? You almost done yet?"

"No," I answered dully. "According to Catherine, we've got nine more confessions to get through if she has seriously killed seventeen people."

"Hey…you okay?"

The concern in his voice unpinned my emotional control. I sobbed the whole story into his ear. "And it's almost eight o'clock and I still haven't heard from Brad," I concluded, sniffling.

"Aw Soph, give him some time, hon. He probably feels like a jackass. You know, I never had any kids," Rick said slowly, "but I always thought of you kind of like a daughter. I guess that's why I've kept you out of the more dangerous things, tryin' to protect you and all. Then I started to feel bad, wanted to give you a shot at a big time story, to help you with your career. Heck, I know you're gonna leave my little paper someday for the big leagues and I guess I have to be okay with that. I'm sorry I sent you into the lion's den, now. You never talked about guys and stuff so I sort of felt safe sending you to talk to a female suspect. I really threw you to the wolves on both scores, didn't I?"

I was touched by his confession and instantly regretted every time I had ever cursed him under my breath or in my head. "No Rick, you didn't do anything wrong. I did. I should never have gotten involved with someone on the job. Now I've jeopardized his position and compromised my own credibility. He shouldn't be messing around with reporters, I knew that. He just made me feel...I don't know. He makes me feel normal," I strove to explain.

"Hey kiddo, let me tell you something. You haven't lost an ounce of credibility with me. Any guy would be lucky to have you. Don't blame yourself. And normal ain't something you're ever going to be so stop trying to find it."

"Gee thanks, Rick. So much for those tender, fatherly moments, huh?"

"Come on, you think I'm stupid? I worked the beat once too. I wasn't always the boss. I know reporters and I know reporting. It's all about observation. I've seen what you can do."

My stomach tightened, along with my grip on the phone. My voice sounded strangled. "What do you mean, Rick?"

"Ease up, Soph. I can practically feel the lightning coming off you from here. And I meant the things you can do. The mind reading, the slammed doors, lights that go on when you enter a room and go off when you leave. Like, you mean to flip the switches but your hand forgets so your head, or whatever it is, fills in for you."

"Are you fucking kidding me? I don't do that!" I could feel panic rising within me, choking me. The lights in the room went dim and I sat in near darkness trying not to hyperventilate.

"Sophia, calm down right now! I mean it," Rick's voice came through the phone faintly, as if from far away, barely audible over the sound of shattering glass. "Now my goddamn whiskey glass is broken and you are gonna hear me out. Get a hold of yourself right fucking now. You hear me? You with me, Sophia?"

His voice was growing louder over the rush of blood in my ears. I made an incoherent sound of assent. I was hearing him. "That's a good girl. Much better. Breathing. In. Out. Okay now here it is. You can do things, Sophia. Not normal things that just anyone can do. When you're distracted, or upset like you are right now, they just happen on their own but I bet if you wanted, you could do them all the time. And that's okay. You hear me? It's okay, hon, it's perfectly fine. Okay? Sophia? Answer me."

"No," I whispered. He heard me anyway.

"Yes, kiddo. I'm right, you know I'm right. Now you can go on denying it after this conversation is over, and I won't bring it up again unless you want to talk about it. But I really think you need to get a handle on this thing and make peace with it. I hate seeing you feel bad all the time. You go around like a ghost of what you could be and I think it's because you are denying this important part of yourself. Frankly, it just tears me up."

I was silent for long minutes, listening to the small, comforting sounds coming through phone: Rick's breathing, him pouring another drink. He let me think a while and then said, "That's all I got for you tonight sweetheart. Keep up the good work. Your pieces are doing well, gaining an audience. Stay as long as you have to for the story. Cut this Brad guy a little slack. And don't forget…you always got me to kick around."

I finally smiled at this last bit. "Thanks, Rick. I mean it. Sorry about your whiskey."

"You should be. That was vintage fucking Glenlivet," he replied, and hung up. I closed my phone and laid back on the bed, thinking about everything he'd said. I was startled out of my reverie by a knock on the door.

"Who is it?" I called, hoping it was Brad but disappointed to hear the busboy reply, "Room service, ma'am."

I got up and pulled open the door, my words about not ordering any room service dying on my lips. The busboy pocketed the twenty Brad held to him and sped away like a frightened deer. Brad stepped forward with a bag of takeout in one hand and a bouquet of more lilies in the other, stargazers this time. He wore a sheepish, sorry expression on his handsome face.

"Um, hey Sophia. I didn't think you'd answer if I called or showed up, so I resorted to stalker tactics."

I didn't say anything. My mind was racing with the best way to handle this and keep my power under control. Part of me was still extremely hurt that he'd basically blamed his whole shitty day on my presence in his prison and his life. The other part was remembering Rick's advice and how I felt about Brad already. Was it too soon to love someone this much? To give them so much power over me? I wondered.

I finally moved aside and said, "Hey, Brad, what's in the bag?"

His relief was nearly palpable. He came in, put the bag and the flowers on the table and strode back to where I stood by the door. He closed it, and pressed me against it. His hands cradled my face, fingers tracing my jaw while he searched my soul with his eyes. I'm sure he found fear and doubt living there. Whatever it was, it caused him to frown. He kissed me, eyes open, watching me. We were at war momentarily, fighting between honesty and forgiveness, lust and love. Brad chose sides first, opting for honesty, and it undid me.

"Sophia," he whispered, "I think I'm in love with you. I know that must seem impossible, or too soon, but it's true. I'm so fucking sorry I took all my problems out on you today. I don't know why I would say any of those things to you. You didn't deserve that from me. I can only ask for you to forgive me and promise if you give me another chance, I will spend my life trying to make it up to you."

Our take out was cold many hours later when we remembered it was sitting on the table still. We ate it anyways. The flowers, however, were still as beautiful as ever and my sleep that night was expansive and dreamless.

****

We were quiet with each other the next morning. It weighed on my mind he'd vowed his love for me but I'd not said anything in return. I worried it upset him and I was awkward, unsure how to respond in kind without sounding stupid. So many things raced through my mind. How would we work out a relationship between us, two different cities, two careers...it seemed impossible. I felt like I was heading for more pain in my life, but couldn't stop myself. The sight of him took my breath away and I caught myself staring more than once, like a schoolgirl mooning over her first crush. Was it just a crush? I doubted the depth of my own feelings and I felt uneasy with myself. He caught me watching him shave, eyes so full of love and desire I felt tears prickling at the back of my eyelids. No, this was no crush.

I must have looked downcast. He came back to the bedroom, shaving completed, and sat on the edge of the bed. "What's wrong, Sophia?" he asked, a worried looking making lines between his azure eyes.

"Oh, nothing. Even though I washed a few things," and he grinned, recalling me washing my undergarments in the shower, which had led to other activities, "I didn't pack enough for more than a week. I'm going to need to go get some clothes soon. I hate shopping," I explained.

His worry lines smoothed. "That's easy to fix. I'll take you shopping when I get off today."

I walked over to where he sat, standing in front of him and looking down at his heartbreakingly handsome face. He wrapped his arms around my hips and gazed up at me with those intense eyes. "You'd do that for me?" I teased a little, trying to lighten my mood.

He was very serious, saying, "I'd do anything to make you happy."

We made it to the prison by nine, but just barely, grabbing coffee and breakfast at my little coffee shop by the hotel. Brad drove fast, joking he couldn't arrest himself. He'd gotten a ride from one of his officers last night, but even after me leaving him there, we still took my rental car. I thought it was a nice show of trust.

Catherine seemed secondary to me now, though she was what had drawn me to Pittsburgh. Brad was all I could think about, all I wanted to think about, and she knew it the second I walked into her cell. She was having none of it; I'd never seen her so angry.

"Did you forget why you are here? Let me give you a hint. It's not to fuck all the cops in town, Sophia. I brought you here! ME! You will listen to what I have to say!" She was screaming at me. All I had done was walk in and sit down, but I was late and she knew why.

"Calm down, Catherine. I'm here now, aren't I?"

"Not in your head, you're not," she spat. "You're with *him*!" She pointed to where Brad stood sentinel by the door. She was right, too; he was a distraction, but I wasn't about to ask him to leave in his own prison. He took care of the problem on his own, though, seeing how worked up she was. He radioed for another officer to take his spot, nodding to me and winking, a move which elicited an actual growl from Catherine's throat. I was grateful for his acuity, happy he wasn't offended but knew what had to be done.

"Happy?" I asked when he'd left. An older officer stood in his place, looking bored.

As per her usual behavior, she ignored my sarcastic comment and switched moods like a radio station turning to another station.

"The ninth raven drew the Hanged Man card. Can you guess how that one died, Sophia?"

"I can only imagine."

"No, you can't. But I'm going to tell you. I drove the hunters' big black truck to a spot near Tyrone and ditched it in an empty parking lot in an old strip mall. I hitched into Tyrone and found a job at a burger joint. The tips were lousy but there was a trailer behind the place the boss, an old lady who smoked like a chimney, said I could stay in as part of my wage. I'd fed her my usual line, battered wife fleeing the abusive husband, and beneath that crusty exterior I could tell a real softie was feeling sorry for me. People are so gullible. I stayed at that job for a while, actually, until spring."

Well that shot my forty two day cycle theory all to hell. She continued, "The dark lord was quiet for a while, resting and working with the Goddess to wake up nature, to produce and create and make the world new again. I felt a slowness within me too, a gathering of strength and stillness. It was very restful."

By my calculations, Catherine would have reached Tyrone by mid-March. I needed to pin down the time of her next kill. "How long would you say you stayed dormant in Tyrone?"

"'Dormant'," she mimicked. "Eager to hear blood, guts and gore? I knew exactly when it was time for the next sacrifice. I felt the dark lord's presence return to my soul at the end of April. A time of rebirth, and a reminder of the death to come. Spring, summer, and fall are only temporary sentinels against winter. It was at the town's Spring Festival that I saw the next raven, waiting on the sidewalk for the parade to end. She was a beautiful girl, Sophia, with long hair as dark as, well...a raven's wing," she guffawed at her own wit.

I was surprised. "A woman? For the Hanged Man card?"

"The card is symbolic, I've told you this," Catherine responded, waxing scholarly again. "It doesn't specifically mean a 'hanged man'. All of the cards carry symbolism. Everything we do can be linked to a symbol of some kind. I try to tie in my sacrifices to the card they've drawn but not every situation is exactly at face value."

"When the...sacrifices...draw their cards, do you mean they literally draw from the deck in some cases, or do you always choose for them? Which comes first, the card or the person you choose to kill?"

Her strange eyes were fathomless. "The dark lord chooses, Sophia, you know that."

Her gaze held mine, hypnotic, like a snake. For the first time, I wondered if there was some way to purposefully pull information from her, using my abilities, without letting her inside of my head any further than she already was. Rick's voice echoed in my head, urging me to embrace my ability.

Her mouth stretched into a wide grin as she read my mind. "You're not strong enough to do both. Which will you choose? Keeping me out, or getting inside?"

My turn to ignore her question. "So, what symbol did the Hanged Man hold for this dark-haired woman?"

"The Hanged Man does depict a man, strung upside down from a wooden beam. Or a cross, if you prefer. It symbolizes not death but martyrdom, or a suspension of some kind. Such as a suspension of belief in order to achieve sainthood. That was the meaning of the card for Mary. I crossed the street that afternoon, my nerves singing after a long time of disuse. She told me her name after I introduced myself and the sound of it zapped me like an electric shock, I felt the dark lord's satisfaction burn in my veins like good liquor. This was the perfect raven for our next sacrifice, his sibilant whisper echoed through my ears. I invited her to the burger shop, offering to make her a milkshake. I said I didn't know many people and thought it would be nice to have a friend to hang out with. I was pathetic, and perfectly believable. She said she'd come by on Friday afternoon. I left, not wanting to push my luck, or creep her out. Plus, I had some preparations to make.

She showed up at the burger place on Friday like she promised. I got her the milkshake I'd promised and we chatted in between customers, getting to know one another. She confessed quite a few things to me, did Mary. I showed her a couple of things, too. Show and tell," Catherine winked.

"What do you mean? Like...witchcraft things? Like you did with Melissa Anselme?"

"Yes, like 'witchcraft things'," she mocked. "I turned the lights off in the diner and then back on again. You know, the weak parlor tricks you can do. She was impressed though. People are so stupid. They need proof of something before they believe it's possible. Mary was not a young, foolish girl but she was no different. She wasn't a young girl, but a mature woman and she'd begun to question her religion. Guess what it was?"

I shook my head, not wanting to play games.

"Spoil sport," she pouted. "Fine I'll tell you. She was Catholic! It was too rich. But her faith was wavering. She was like a fallen woman. I changed all that quickly," she smiled her cat-like grin, full of herself. "She called me a witch and a demon, insisting on praying for my soul, right there in the burger shop. Down on her knees, worshipping some white, long-haired hippie dude that never helped anyone, far as I can tell."

"Gee Catherine, didn't that hurt? Even burn a little, praying to God?"

"Very funny. Don't you listen? I'm not evil. I'm not Satanic or any of that shit. I'm merely the darker side of the natural world." She licked her lips and leaned forward. "Want to know how I killed her?"

"Not especially," I replied, knowing she was going to tell me no matter what I said.

"I lured her to my trailer with the promise of some good old-fashioned prayer," she grinned. "Mary was gonna save my witch ass single-handedly and help me enter the kingdom of heaven. She kept on praying when we got there, on her knees in the living room until the sleeping pills I fed her in that milkshake kicked in. I tied a rope around her ankles so I could hang her upside down but couldn't really think where to do it until inspiration struck. The Catholic Church of course!"

"Wait a minute...you hung her upside down inside a church? Where did you do this, in Tyrone?" "Don't jump ahead!" Catherine snapped at me. "I *wanted* to hang her from the Catholic Church but the stupid priest lives there and besides, it's practically in the middle of town. I would totally have gotten caught. I was lucky she'd driven to the burger shop in a car, one of those Outback things, so I could stash her in the back of it and take her someplace secluded.

"Tyrone is famous for railroads, so I thought I'd do something with that. I hauled her out to one of those railway bridges and tied her feet to the track. I had to do the circle and blood ritual on the tracks, which sucked. She started to come around so I acted quickly, slitting her throat with my big knife and then throwing her over the side of the bridge. I peeked over the edge and watched her for a while. She hung there bleeding out and twitching for a really long time. Then I left. I assume, when the next train came, the rope was severed by the wheels and her body dumped into the water underneath the bridge. Only 'God' knows where she is now," Catherine finished, her pleasure in her own pun a horrible thing to behold.

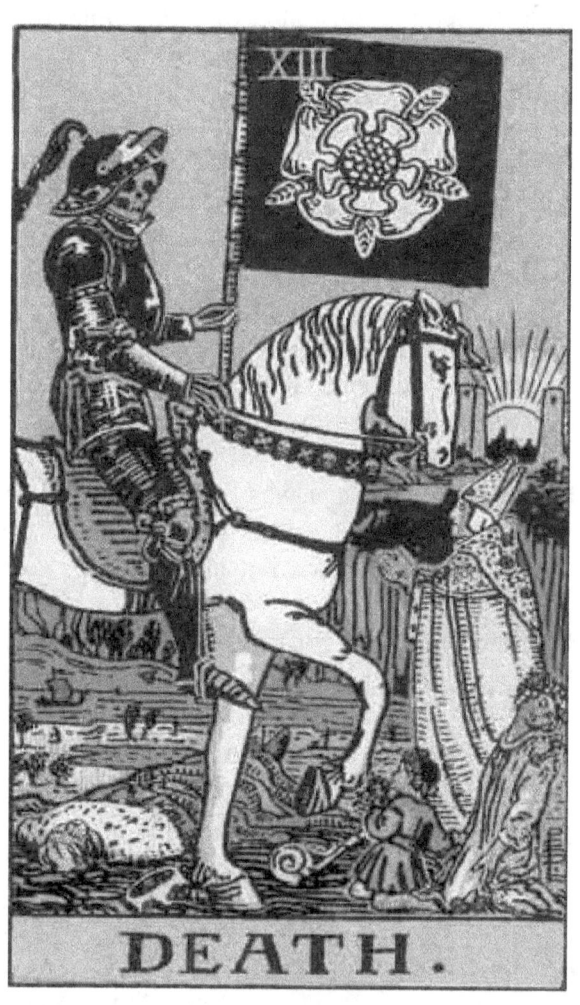

13-Death

As usual," the Raven Witch Killer continued, "I stole the car and got the hell out of there."

"Worried about God's retribution?" I asked facetiously.

"You wish!" she crowed. "I don't know how people like you and I can ever embrace a god like that. Maybe you'll tell me when we're done here."

"I doubt a degenerate like you could understand," I answered. I was having trouble with that belief myself, trying to reconcile a deity who let this woman live. In spite of myself, I was beginning to embrace the idea the other part of my legacy, the wilder side that did not demand rhyme or reason for the forces of nature or the presence of evil, was maybe the right side. I knew she could hear my thoughts and for once I didn't care. I could hear her too, now. Her happiness buzzed in my brain like a sickness until I concentrated and shut her out.

"Questioning your faith is not shameful, Sophia. All humans suffer from an existential need to believe in something greater than themselves. That I have found proof of my dark lord's love should not sway another from their path. I chose you because I knew you were like me, and I refuse to be judged by a lesser creature than my own peer. Whichever side you choose, now, makes no difference. You have the same power I do, and you believe even if you choose not to admit it, therefore you are fit to be my judgment and that means I have nearly won my goal."

"I judged you long before now, Catherine. I judged you to be an evil bitch who deserved to burn in hell for what you've done."

"Heaven and hell are Christian concepts," she replied, sounding disappointed in me. "I seek only true judgment. You, as my peer, as a fellow witch, will provide it, so my work may then be presented to my dark lord as completed and so my name will live on to bring honor to Him."

"You won't get that from me. I'll write your story and then everyone will forget you once the initial horror has died out. You'll just be another psychotic raving lunatic in time."

She gritted her teeth. "We'll see."

"So what's next? If I'm guessing correctly, it's the Death card, am I right?"

She sat in stony silence. I said, "Actually, I believe that card only signifies true death if it's in the reversed position. In the upright position, it can signify rebirth or some sort of transition..."

She refused to speak, staring at the walls of her cell. Shit. I had to get her talking again and in light of her recent diatribe about what I was and what she was, I came up with an idea on the spot. I knew the surveillance camera was watching and so did she, but I leaned forward anyway and touched the handcuffs on her wrists, half convinced it wouldn't work. But it did. Her handcuffs unlocked themselves and fell away; I felt a surge of sheer power course through me and I was elated at my success in controlling my ability to perform a task on purpose. Catherine rubbed her wrists and stared hard at me before breaking into a huge, delighted smile, winking at me like I was her fellow conspirator.

I heard the guard gasp in fear and amazement at the cell door, heard him muttering urgently into his radio and knew our time was short for the day. Brad would be down here any minute to put the cuffs back on and haul me out of there. The door guard would never come in here by himself, unless she was killing me. It was against the rules. Brad would be pissed.

"Naughty, naughty, Sophia," she teased with a gleam in her eye. "Let me tell you quickly about Death before Daddy comes to spank you. The raven chosen to honor the Death card, in the *reversed* position, I might add, as a small child. A baby, actually."

I closed my eyes in pain. "Look at me!" she hissed, grabbing my arm. The contact joined my consciousness with hers and I saw through her eyes how the Death card's promise had been fulfilled.

A small, innocent baby, chubby arms and blue eyes stared at me/Catherine from its little seat in the grocery cart. Catherine's/my arms reached for the baby and snatched it from the cart, tucking its soft green blankets around it and holding it tight to her/my chest. The mother's back was turned, the stupid woman staring at a selection of deli meats and paying no attention to her baby. One minute there, gone the next. Leaving the grocery store, a sign reading "Hunker General Store" dwindling behind us, we sped away to the forest green Outback waiting in the parking lot. We placed the baby on the passenger's seat and arranged the seatbelt around its tiny body. It wasn't apparent if the baby was a boy or a girl. I could feel Catherine's thought that the dark lord demanded innocence and so she took it, no matter what form it was. We drove to a secluded spot behind a rest stop just off the freeway and entered a wooded area. We cast the circle with handfuls of salt from our pocket and blood from our wrist, and placed the baby in the middle. It waved its chubby arms and legs in the air, tiny fists clenched.

I felt tears streaming down my cheeks and a burning pain where her claw-like hand clenched my arm, forcing the link between us to remain open so I could see what she saw. My mind rejected the images painted in my brain, vehemently denying what I was seeing. I heard a commotion at the cell door as if from far away but I was hypnotized by her eyes and something inside me screamed that I must bear witness to the baby's death.

The infant began crying, the cooling June air cold on its fragile skin. I cut my arm in a different spot to get the blood flowing again, Catherine's arm, and drew the raven symbol on the baby's chest. It liked that, smiling at me with its wide eyes and toothless grin. I cooed at it for a moment with Catherine's voice before covering its nose and mouth with my hand, cutting off its air. The baby struggled briefly, like a bird with a broken wing...straining for air, trying so hard to live...

Our connection was broken when Brad's voice shouted, "What the fuck? Let her go you sick bitch!" He reached her side and she reared back, letting go of me and appearing ready to strike at him like a snake. He was taking no chances. He hit her with a Taser, stunning her so that the two officers charging in behind him could re-cuff her.

He turned to me, eyes blazing with fear and fury. He didn't say anything to me. He hauled me from my chair and half-carried me to his office. I knew he was enraged at the risk I'd taken, possibly even afraid of what I'd done. He was shaking, the hair on his muscular arms raised where his white dress shirt was rolled up. He stared at me like I was...well, a witch. Something evil, to be feared.

I was still crying for the loss of the baby's life, the shared memory of its death galloping through my brain over and over again. My abilities were growing too strong since I'd acknowledged them, or she was much stronger than I'd thought. Either way I'd seen too much. The fear and anguish in Brad's eyes were too much to bear. I sank to the floor and buried my head in my arms, dying inside.

After a moment, I felt his hands on me, gathering me in his arms. He told his staff he was leaving early and to call him no matter what if anything untoward happened, holding me upright and stuffing me in the rental car. He drove me to the hotel, asking me questions and peering at me with that worried look on his face. I was so tired, though, I wanted to sleep so badly that it was hard to concentrate on his words.

He led me up to the room, letting us in. He undressed and bathed me, then wrapped me in a blanket from the bed. "Sophia? Where's your phone sweetheart?"

I gestured vaguely to my purse. He fished it out. I dimly heard him talking to someone but couldn't muster the will to eavesdrop. He hung up and put the phone aside, undressing quickly and joining me on the bed. He pulled me against him, his back resting against the headboard. "Sophia," he whispered in my ear, "come back to me."

I wanted to but something about what happened between Catherine and I had drained me completely. The look I'd seen in his eyes sent me from one extreme to another, from anguish and fear to heartbreak and dejection. I couldn't seem to swim my way out of any of it.

Brad started talking to me about his life. We'd had long, heartfelt talks before but this was different, deeply personal. He told me about his childhood, a happy one, and his parents, who loved each other until they died.

"They were older when they had me," he explained. His voice was soothing, his chest rumbling beneath me. "I was a surprise."

He kept talking until I felt something inside me break free from its moorings, no longer bound by the crushing weight of the baby's death and the crevasse in our relationship.

"How did they die?" I asked finally. He clutched me tighter but didn't otherwise acknowledge my return to the land of the living. "Old age, actually. They died in bed, first Mom and then Dad a couple weeks later. They're buried out on the property. They loved that place so much, I had to get permission but that's where they are."

"What did you do after they died?"

"I moved around for a few months, then decided to go to college. I was nineteen when they died, so not too late for school. I landed in Harrisburg and decided to be a cop."

"Why? Was your dad a cop?"

I could feel his smile, hear it in his voice. "No, he was a tour guide, offering trail riding on horseback through Amish country. He was too gentle for the harshness of police work."

I learned he'd been married once. He met her in college. She was his literature professor and thirteen years his senior. "No one in class paid much attention to her at first. She was just another teacher, you know? College kids don't always think of their professors as actual people.

"Then, that spring, she started to change from this frumpy older lady to a beautiful woman. Of course, she had been all along, but we shallow youths didn't notice until she bloomed before our eyes. She came in one day with her hair down, instead of up in a bun as usual, and one of the girls asked her where she had gotten her hair done. She said nowhere, it always looked like that, and the girl said she looked beautiful, which is what we were all thinking. I'll never forget what she said." I looked up at him to see his mouth quirk as he recited: "In winter's cloak, I hide away; retreat inside my safest day; until the breath of spring appears; brings away those shadowed years; youth's visage, it never stays, yet holds the eye; in light, it stays."

"That's lovely," I said, and meant it.

"It was lovely and so was she. At least two of her male students asked her out before the end of class that day but she shot them down, saying she didn't date students. So I waited until I graduated and then asked her out, pointing out I wasn't a student anymore."

"And she went for it?"

"Hell no. But I was persistent and I wore her down. She finally agreed, with great reluctance, to coffee in the cafeteria. We were married a year later and a year after that, she was gone."

"I'm so sorry." I snuggled closer, offering comfort.

He rubbed my arm where it lay across his chest. "So, I moved back here, fixed up the old homestead, and waited around for you to show up." He kissed my forehead, eyes full of ocean waves of sadness and love. I answered the look in the only way possible, with my body and my soul.

In the afterglow of our lovemaking, the dark stillness of night, I admitted out loud what I feared to say in daylight."

"I can...do things. Like *her*." There was no mistaking who I meant.

"I know," Brad's answer echoed in the darkened room.

"Are you afraid of me?"

He sighed. "I'll never be afraid of you."

"But you were, weren't you? I saw, at the prison, you were scared of me." Tears filled my eyes.

He pulled me up, noses and foreheads touching, only the pale light of the moon filtering through the sheer curtains revealing the whites of his eyes and the flash of his teeth. "I was never afraid of you, Sophia," he whispered. "I'm afraid for you."

He kissed me tenderly, twice, before whispering, "I love you."

We slept then, one in peaceful slumber and the other tormented by blue, blood-streaked corpses of infants, dressed in clothing made of ink black raven's feathers.

14-Temperance

Before returning to the prison later the next day, Brad took me shopping for new clothes as he'd promised. There was a distance between us now, a wedge somehow caused by the events of the preceding day. I was confused. He said he loved me, but today he acted as though I was a stranger. I know he'd spoken to Rick. My cell phone showed a phone call last night when I was...unable to function briefly. What had Rick said to him? I vowed to find out later.

I went through the motions of choosing items of clothing mechanically. *It wasn't the fun outing either of us imagined the day before*, I thought. We went back to the hotel to drop my new things off and so I could change. He let me out at the entrance, saying he had work to do and that he'd see me when I got there. I watched him drive away in his Jeep, laden with bags and a heavy heart.

I dragged my feet getting ready, calling Rick a few times and getting voicemail each time. I didn't arrive at the prison until noon, well past my typically early arrival time of nine in the morning. The group of ravens--a conspiracy, my brain supplied, how apt-- increased to ten. One was smaller than the rest, a fledgling with downy feathers ruffling in the breeze. I felt bile rise to the back of my throat at the significance of an infant among their ranks.

Brad was not waiting for me on the steps. I sort of suspected he wouldn't be after the morning's shopping debacle. I slumped forward in my seat, resting my forehead on the steering wheel.

For a moment, I considered just quitting, heading back to Philly, back to my life and my empty apartment, where the cupboard doors opened and closed without human hands touching them, according to my subconscious whims. Where my bed sat, cold as iron. Briefly, I wondered if I were a witch, why couldn't I just spell myself not to love him, or for him not to love me, or to love all of me, even the abnormal parts. Of course, I knew the answer, either by instinct or some other means. Love is a force of nature, uncontrolled and uncontrollable.

Wearily, I climbed from the car and slammed the door, consigning myself to another day in the presence of evil. Not before I had it out with Brad once and for all, I decided right then. I remembered painfully how much of a shadow I'd been before I met Brad, before any of this happened. I thought of what Rick said, how he didn't want to see me just trying to be like everyone else, wearing 'normal' like it was ill-fitting clothing. I would not be that girl, slogging wearily through life and pretending to be something I wasn't! I shed my apathy like a discarded robe. I was going to fight for what I wanted, dammit. No cold, lonely bed and no more denying what I was. I would have my way. I wrenched open the double wood doors and strode down the hallway to Brad's office door, yanking it open and all but hurtling inside. He stood by his desk, his handsome face wearing an astonished expression.

I rushed over to him and wrapped myself around him, searing his lips with my own. He buried his hands in my hair and crushed my mouth with the force of his emotions but I didn't care. I broke contact only when I could no longer breathe, "I love you."

The force of my oath rippled through the air, pulling books from the shelves and knocking papers to the floor where they swirled in intricate dances before settling in random patterns around the room. It brushed through his hair and brightened all the colors in the room, making his eyes glow like blue stars. The oath tore through me, proclaiming my body and soul as his. We stood together, bound by love, as though we dwelled in the eye of a powerful storm. He never flinched, accepting all of me in that instant. His choice, his fate, his destiny...sealed with mine forever.

****

"I'll be right there at the cell door the whole time," Brad said as we slowly made our way to Catherine's cell. "She's been quiet all night, the swing and grave shifts told me earlier. Plus I've got some news from Yoakum, and the lawyer finally called to say the psychiatrist will be here tomorrow. We're getting somewhere, honey, just keep hanging in there, but absolutely no more antics like what you pulled yesterday." He glared at me, a little, which reminded me of my stupidity from the day before. He couldn't be too mad at me though...I'd just pledged my life, my soul, to his. It still glowed in his eyes, blinding me. I can see that now.

"She can mind-fuck me all day without touching me, if she wants," I said, frustrated. I needed to be able to repeat yesterday in some way. If I could find exact body locations, we could get the ball rolling on this bitch. "You know there are more ravens on the gate every day. What the fuck are they doing there? Do you think she's calling them, somehow?"

"Honey, just promise. It's not worth losing your mind to her. Stay out of her reach. I don't know how to help you with...well, the parts I don't really understand. I know that after she touched you, you went into shock and then you were nearly catatonic for hours. You're no use to yourself, me, or this investigation in that condition," he pleaded.

"Okay. I promise I'll stay away from her. Hey," I stopped him before he could keep walking. "What did Rick say when you called him yesterday?"

"He told me to give you space to figure things out on your own and that he'd never heard your voice so full of love as when you spoke my name."

In full view of his officers, I kissed him soundly and he kissed me back. We were reckless. I fully believed our oath of love would protect us both.

I tried to put the past twenty-four hours out of my mind and concentrate on the task at hand, getting through another session with Catherine. I felt invincible, as if there was nothing Catherine could do to me now, with Brad's love bolstering me, giving me strength. I have never been so wrong.

She launched straight into confession mode when I entered her cell, to my surprise. I'd expected some type of commentary on my personal life, but I barely had time to sit before her voice rang out, loud and clear and determined.

"Temperance was a two raven card," she began. Her eyes were closed as she spoke. I could see her eyeballs rolling wildly in their sockets beneath the delicate skin of her eyelids, thin blue veins tracing the porcelain skin. This was a new tactic. My voice recorder, returned by Brad, was rolling in my pocket but I was glad for the video camera in the corner, capturing this odd behavior. She looked as though she were a young child reciting an oft told story, or catechism. I shifted in my seat, uneasy. Something was wrong.

"Catherine?" I made her name a question. "Are you okay?"

"Two ravens, flapping aimlessly around in Rainsburg," she intoned. "But it wasn't raining, not then. It was summer, and beautiful. I ran out of gas a ways from town but I didn't mind. I started walking up the shoulder of the highway and it wasn't too long before two guys in a beat up green Ford pickup stopped for me, offered me a ride. I had to sit in the cab between them, their meaty thighs touching mine on either side. It was disgusting," the murderess shuddered delicately, eyes still closed.

"They talked a lot, those two. Cawing, true ravens. Ravens and crows are called *corvids*, did you know? My two corvids were forty years old, both of them, they told me. They were twins, the fraternal kind, not the identical kind. When I heard that I heard, too, the excited whisper of the dark lord's glee echoing through me. 'Temperance', he sang and I found later that was indeed the card the brothers drew. They were oblivious, talking one after the other. I remember their names because of that book. I'm not stupid, you know." This last was said with some heat, as if she had gleaned my assessment of her intelligence level. And of course, she had.

I tried anyway. "I know you're not stupid. What book, Catherine? Were they named for characters in a book? And why aren't you looking at me?"

"So much power today," she whispered, giggling like a naughty child. Her eyelids did not flutter from their closed position, however, and I shifted in my seat.

"The book is where their mom got the idea for their names. The one driving was Jules, a big guy with a barrel chest and a short beard. Handsome, I guess, if you like that sort of thing. Does Officer Shaw have a big cock, Sophia?"

"That's none of your business. We've been over this, Catherine. What was the other twin's name?"

"Do you love it, what he does to you? His hands on you while he stuffs himself inside..."

"Catherine, I'm done talking about that. It's frankly beneath you and insulting to me. Now, your lawyer is coming here tomorrow with a psychiatrist to analyze you. Most likely they will move to deem you unfit to stand trial. I will be required to hand over my tapes and our conversations here will be through. I will also probably never be able to speak to you again. Do you have a story to finish or would you prefer to dwell on my sex life?" My voice raised, I slammed my hand down on the table's surface for emphasis. It stung my palm but the instant she finally opened her eyes, my pain was forgotten and replaced by fear. Adrenaline spiked through me like a shot of caffeine.

Her oddly beautiful green-blue splotched eyes had been replaced with orbs of pure black, like the pupil had leaked and oozed into the surface of her eyes, leaving no color behind. They sparkled beneath the harsh fluorescent bulb like polished bits of onyx. I gasped involuntarily, then screamed and covered my mouth when next she spoke.

"You will listen to what I have to say, white witch," Catherine boomed in a voice that was not her own. No longer musical, like the voice of a siren, what issued forth from her shapely mouth was deep, dragged over shards of glass, and bleeding with contempt and darkness. Her black eyes pierced me, pinning me to my spot.

From my peripheral vision, I could see Brad draw his gun. I watched Catherine's head move in his direction and I knew I needed to get control of the situation.

"Catherine! Tell me about the other twin!" I shouted.

Her head turned back to me, empty eyes regarding me with a phantom's watchful gaze filled with void. I felt like an insect pinned to a specimen board. I concentrated on increasing my own calmness, using my power to shield myself as I had before and slow my heartbeat. Radiating good energy, I used my gift with purpose, unsure if I was doing any good but desperate to block out fear and finish this for good.

I was marginally successful because when Catherine next spoke, her voice was her own, though her eyes remained black and fathomless.

"The other one was hideous, a deformed freak. His name was Verne. Get it? Jules and Verne? He looked like one of those creatures. What were those creatures called?"

I hesitated. "Which creatures?"

"You know, the ones in the ground...the guy found them when he went there in his time machine. What were they called?"

"I think you mean the book called 'The Time Machine' but it was written by H.G. Wells, not Jules Verne."

She sounded crestfallen. "Jules Verne didn't write that one?"

"No, he did write other things though. He wrote *20,000 Leagues Under the Sea* and..."

Catherine started banging her head hard against the wooden surface of the table. Alarmed, I stood up and reached for her. I was stopped by a shout from Brad. "SOPHIA! NO!"

I stopped. So did she. She raised her head, blood running from a cut on her forehead and mingling with tears streaming from her eyes. The bloody tears pooled on her chin and dripped, pat, pat, pat, onto the tabletop.

"I *am* stupid! You were right. I can't even get the damn books right!" she sobbed.

Incredibly I found myself comforting her. "No, you're not stupid. Those are hard books to get through. I never even read *20,000 Leagues* myself."

Her tone was hopeful, mitigated somewhat by the creepy blacked out eyes. "Really?"

"I swear it. Do...do you want to tell me what happened to the twins?"

"Okay," she sniffled and wiped her nose with her prison uniform sleeve, handcuffs rattling. Her eyes were still black, no hint of color bleeding back into their centers. "So, they picked me up, and I had the Temperance card, and they were so 'out of balance' it wasn't even funny. You know what I mean? Like the longer I rode with them, the more I noticed how Jules had gotten all the good stuff and Verne got all the shit. It didn't seem right. I decided to fix it. Fixing nature's mistake was like an in your face moment to the Goddess and the dark lord seemed to really like that idea.

I told them a sad story about how I was starting over because my baby had died and the daddy left me after it happened. I said I'd decided to just get in the car and go as far as I could and wherever I stopped is where I'd get a fresh new life.

"Verne said a lot of nice things, like, "Oh you poor thing!' and 'I can't believe any man would leave a pretty thing like you!" "And right when you needed him the most!"

"Jules waited until his brother ran out of steam and then he said, "You got no place to stay and no job yet. Plus your car's run outta gas. You'd best stay with us a spell until you get your feet under you."

"Normally, I'd never agree to stay with two strange men but they had this thing about them. Some kind of aura I couldn't really make out, and I'm pretty good with auras and reading thoughts and stuff like that. Maybe you noticed?

"Anyway. It was like they was two nice grizzly bears that came out of the woods and decided to be people."

Catherine's demeanor and tone changed entirely, adopting a country twang, her inflection and grammar becoming completely different than normal. It was like she was putting on a new persona and it rattled me.

"I said okay," she continued, "and they both just beamed at me like I was a new pet or something. They chatted back and forth in that way they had, one starting a sentence and the other finishing it. Jules drove us to their house, which was a real nice place, settled back in the woods a ways. We had to bump down a dirt lane for a while to get to it and it was super-hot, the end of June almost. Verne and his monster face showed me to a spare bedroom when we got there. It was nice, kinda plain. There was a bed with a quilt on it and a nightstand, nothing fancy. But it was real homey. It had its own bathroom, which was a huge plus.

"I just sort of stayed a while. Jules went back for my car the next day and put some gas in it. He parked it by his truck and never said another word about it. I don't know if he went through it to find info on me, which wouldn't have helped because I threw everything out that wouldn't match my story."

"Catherine, who did you tell them you were? I mean, what name do you give your victims? Do you make one up, or tell them the truth?"

"Oh I always tell them my real name. It's where part of the power comes from. There is great power in a name, you know that Sophia. Stop interrupting," she scolded. "So anyway, both twins just took me at face value and took me in. As the days went on I sort of felt affection for the big goofs. They were like the brothers I'd never had. Even Verne with his fucked up face and slow ways was kind of sweet.

We settled into a routine. Both the guys worked at a paper mill just outside of town, and I cleaned and cooked meals. They never said a word about me looking for a job, and I never did make it in to town. They never had nobody come visit them. Both their parents was dead like mine and yours, Sophia. They told me the people at work were okay but not too trustworthy. The other guys at the mill made fun of Verne sometimes, which Jules didn't like.

"It was real domestic. They never tried nothing gross either. Like I said, we were all like brothers and sister. I really grew to love them."

She was crying again, absently, not bothering to wipe her cheeks where the salt traced silver tracks down her smooth skin. Her black eyes were still hollow, overflowing endlessly.

"You really did," I said, aghast. I could feel it coming off of her in waves, buffeting against my zone of protection. Her grief was nearly tangible, like tar coating me. I tasted bitterness, the flavor of crushed aspirin, poisonous on my tongue. I saw what she would say in that aftertaste left in my mouth, before she even spoke.

"Arsenic kills slowly, over time. It's a man-made poison, though the material comes from the earth. It is therefore forbidden to me, but nature provides. Foxglove kills nearly instantly, but it's messy. Other herbs and plants can kill slowly but need large amounts and taste bitter." She smiled, knowingly. I gagged and shook my head, trying to clear the phantom poison from my taste buds.

"Hemlock," she forged on with her lesson, "kills very quickly and is almost tasteless. It is a gentle death too. The victim feels cold and then the body shuts off nearly at once after that."

As she spoke, a chill crept into the room. It spread from my feet upward. I fought it off, envisioning crackling fires and the heat of the August sun. She kept talking, ignoring my growing distress. I could feel her in my mind, searching for me so she could feed from my emotions of fear and loathing.

"I loved my twins. I didn't want them to suffer. It doesn't take much hemlock to kill a grown man, but I took no chances. I collected it under the full moon and made an infusion. I put the entire batch into their iced tea with a particularly nice dinner. Fried chicken, garlic mashed potatoes, and roasted corn on the cob. Both boys loved that meal," she said the last to herself, but continued at once.

"They went real quiet when the hemlock hit their bodies. Verne didn't understand what was happening to him but he said he was cold and wanted to lie down. I tucked him in his bed and covered him up with a bunch of blankets. He asked for a song, so I sang him 'Twinkle,

Twinkle, Little Star' and then I told him I needed to go check on his brother."

My body began to thaw just as a gust of wind blew through the barren cell, blowing her magnificent hair around her face in a corona of fire. I heard Brad shout in surprise and then call for backup on his radio. I focused on Catherine. She was no longer crying but by her voice sounded as pissed as I'd ever heard her.

"Jules was nearly dead when I got back to the dining room, lying on the floor under the table. He couldn't speak by then but he managed to grab me by the throat and nearly choke me to death. After everything I'd done for him and his ugly brother! He finally died, leaving bruises all over my neck that took weeks to fade away.

I had to get the hand truck from the garage to move Jules into his brother's room, and then pull Verne off the bed onto the floor next to Jules. I undressed them and found that neither of them had all the right man parts. Someone had cut off their balls at some point in their lives, both of them. That explained why they never tried to jump my bones, I guess. I worried though that their incompleteness meant they weren't going to be a good enough sacrifice, that I'd killed them for nothing. I guess it didn't matter though because I heard the dark lord telling me to balance their lives back in June when I first met them so I went ahead with my ritual. I used Jules's chainsaw to cut them both in half lengthwise. Boy was that messy! I cut them right down the middle as neat as I could. Half a nose, half a chest, half arm and leg. I let each of them keep their man parts, what they had left anyway. I figured they had suffered enough in that department. Plus I didn't want to touch those nasty things. They were like brothers to me. It would be just wrong.

"I sewed each half of a brother to the other half. That was the balancing part. I had to use an ice pick to make the holes and wax string to bind them together, so it wasn't very pretty. Plus it took forever and it was really freaking hot in the house. Also, I had to do it twice, front and back, for each brother."

"I'm sure you did the best you could for them," I said, numb. The chilling cold and the windy theatrics had left. All that remained was two women, each with her own demons, facing each other across a wooden table. Brad and the other officers blocked the cell door, two facing the hall but casting fearful looks into the cell at the Raven Witch Killer, hearing every word from her twisted and beautiful mouth.

She brightened at my words. "I did! I really did try my best. I'm sure they would have appreciated my efforts. Now they were perfectly balanced, you see? Smart and dumb. Handsome and ugly. I cast my circle around them because I was too exhausted to move them to a cleaner spot. I cut my legs, each one, to draw the raven on their chests. I broke the circle when the ritual was complete and packed up all the nice things they'd bought me."

"What kinds of things did they buy you?"

"Clothes, makeup, books, stuffed toys...you know, things. Damn Sophia, hasn't anyone ever bought you anything before?" She was annoyed again.

"Sorry. What did you do next?"

"I loaded up Jules's truck. I figured the cops might be looking for the Outback, so I left it even though I didn't want to. I liked that car. The next thing I did was douse the bodies and the house with gasoline, like the history guy's house and his dead meat. I lit that sucker on fire and got the hell out of there. I wanted to give the twins a decent burial but that was the best I could do for them," she added, slipping back into melancholy with the ease of an eel through water.

"So where did your dark lord send you next?"

"We went to Mount Union." *Her use of the plural 'we' is a good indicator of just how crazy she is*, I thought.

I was surer than ever Catherine Meara would never see the inside of a courtroom. I was right, of course, but for different reasons.

"What did you do in Mount Union?"

"We paid a visit to the devil."

15-The Devil

Excuse me? You and your 'Horned God' visited the devil?" I smirked. Her story was weak in the dark lord department, in my book. I didn't doubt she believed what she was saying, but like many serial killers who hear voices, her recollection of these conversations was spotty at best. *A god described as wearing horns visiting the devil is almost too ironic for even her to believe*, I thought. She scared me, I admitted it as much, a long time before we came to the devil part of her story. I was rapidly becoming a believer in the rhetoric she was spouting and for a lifelong Catholic, a reorganization of religious beliefs at the hands of a serial killer was frightening at best. I hated her for making me face that part of me I'd suppressed for so long.

Instead of anger or scorn, she just simpered at me. "Isn't it deliciously ironic? Imagine my surprise when the devil card chose a woman to be his raven. Oh, the dark lord has such a light-hearted sense of humor!"

"You chose another woman for your next victim? What was her name, did you know?"

"*We* did not *choose* the raven, Sophia. The cards chose the ravens and the dark lord sanctioned their sacrifices. No, I never knew her name. I was in a hurry, trying to get somewhere before the Autumnal Equinox. I had something special planned on that particular September 22nd." Her haughty superiority had returned, having shed that hick routine once the twins were a distant memory. She still had shiny streaks on her face where she'd cried for them, and I knew her grief was real though it was now long forgotten. She was ready to show off some more. But her story gaps were starting to piss me off.

"So, you missed Spring Equinox, Beltane even, and both Solstices, but Autumnal Equinox was an emergency?" I shook my head in disbelief. "Didn't you tell me you didn't plan any of these things? The dark lord commanded and you bowed down like his bitch was what I've gotten from these stories."

"Who says I missed any of those holidays?" Her sly cat grin didn't work as well with empty, soulless eyes. The void in them served to emphasize my point, making her seem like a marionette whose strings were manipulated by an amateur. She continued, saying, "We both know why the Autumnal Equinox is most important."

My spine stiffened. I'd forgotten the importance of September in the midst of all her craziness. "It was the month my parents were killed in a car accident."

"You sure it was an accident? Better check on that, Sophia," she whispered. "And ye-eesss...it is a month which prepares for death. My parents met their end the same year and month as yours did. But I can promise you, theirs was no accident." She grinned wickedly.

"But, you were just a child!" There was no way she could have killed her parents at nine years old and gotten away with it...was there?

"Children hear the light and the dark in equal measure. Why do you think your grandmother never taught you as soon as she knew what you were? Why do you think she insisted on drowning your power in Catholic bullshit?"

She drummed her fingers on the table top. I didn't care to dwell in the past with her, and certainly not to question my Nonna's motives with a killer, so I said, "What happened when you found the next victim?"

She gave me those blank eyes for a moment. "It was only mid-August but like I said, I was in a hurry. I found her by accident. She was walking along the side of the road and dressed in very little. I mean, is there modesty left in the world? She had blond dyed hair, all sprayed and teased.

She was wearing tall red heels, totally inappropriate for walking. They were what I like to call 'hooker shoes'. She stuck out a manicured thumb when she heard my truck. I could feel the Devil card insisting on fulfillment and the dark lord agreed she would do as the next raven. I stopped on the shoulder and she jumped in the passenger side.

She had perfect makeup, fake boobs, and plucked or shaved bits of skin showing everywhere. She was a disgusting whore!" Catherine's voice was laced with acid contempt.

"Was this Neve Ramirez?" I asked suddenly, thinking perhaps the teen had incensed Catherine with skimpy clothing and over sexual tones. It was clear that sex was a hot button topic for her, but then I thought it through and answered my own question. "No, wait. It couldn't be her, could it...the timeframe doesn't match, and Neve had brown hair. I suppose she could have bleached it..."

Catherine elaborated. "That girl disappeared up by Sunbury, remember? I didn't get to Sunbury until the day I turned myself in."

I came to a realization. "You didn't have anything to do with Neve Ramirez, did you?"

"Of course not," she shrugged. "I read about her disappearance in the paper when I blew into town and used it to get myself where I needed to be. Right here with you." She winked at me.

I shook it off and forged ahead. "Okay. So what happened after the blonde got in the truck?"

"The Devil card is a duality, or symbiosis, of sorts," she responded, using her scholarly persona again. "It represents bondage and materialism. Or, bondage *because* of materialism. I could see why the hooker in heels girl fit the card. All she cared about was her lost phone, the condition of her clothes, how she needed a new manicure...she never stopped talking about herself or her appearance. All I could do was nod in the appropriate places, as my input was not required. She droned on and on about a fight with her boyfriend, saying, 'How is it my fault that guys like to look at me?' She was a slave to keeping up her looks. She bragged about how she got a lot of different men to buy her things. She'd said, 'Look at these,' and grabbed her own boobs. 'You think I could afford these babies on my own?' and then laughed about tricking some idiot into paying for them. I could not wait for the opportunity to kill that bitch.

"I asked her where she was going and where she came from, but she was very vague. I had the idea from something I read in her thoughts that she'd done something criminal she was trying to get away from. Stealing money from some guy, I thought. She said she was going wherever I was headed and where she came from was in the past and so it didn't matter anyway. I said I was going to Mechanicsburg. She said that was fine with her. Of course, she never made it to Mechanicsburg. She only made it a few miles west of Mount Union. I pulled off on a national forest road, saying I needed to pee. She was all for stopping so she could fuck with her hair some more. I've never met anyone so vain in my life!"

"I parked near the port-a potties and checked for other cars or hikers. Even though it was summer time, most of the crowd would be near the water, trying to cool off in the heat if possible. This particular rest area wasn't terribly close to the water and not too close to the main road either. It was perfect. As always, the dark lord provided.

I got out of the truck and pulled the tire iron out of the back as she was getting out of the passenger side. I held it down and behind me a bit, not that she noticed. I followed her as she headed for the john, lugging her giant purse full of hair supplies and makeup. She got in one of the little toilet cubicles and I followed right behind, crowding and pushing her inside. I locked the door behind us. She must have been use to sharing facilities because she didn't ask questions about why I was in the cramped and smelly room with her. She just asked if I wanted to go first. I shook my head and she peeled off her holey shorts, no underwear I noticed to my disgust, and plopped down on the toilet seat. She started to open her mouth as her stream was released from her body, but I brought the tire iron down on the top of her skull and shut her up quickly. She didn't even scream out. I think she welcomed release from her bondage to herself. I beat her over and over with the tire iron, across her head, her face, her neck, and her stupid fake ass tits. She didn't try to fight back or defend herself. I hated her for that."

"So...you beat her to death in a port-a-potty?" I was incredulous. She'd confessed to some of the most brutal and cruel acts I'd ever heard of, but this was unreal. Besides, it was less methodical than I was used to hearing from her. It smacked of desperation.

"Yes, I did. I cast the circle all around the thing, on the outside, and drew the raven all over her squishy implants. They felt like play dough," she mused. "Then I dumped her body into the hole and left."

"Wasn't there blood everywhere? You would have had to have been covered in it."

"Not really. After the first whack, she kind of slumped backward, up against the rear cube wall. I think most of the blood went down the piss hole. I had a little bit on me, but nothing too noticeable. The most blood I saw came from my wrist, where I cut it with my knife to draw the raven symbol."

"Did you keep her purse, or go through it to find out who she was?"

"Why would I keep that? I didn't need make up or hair crap. Besides, I don't care who they are, mostly. She was just an easy way to fulfill the promise of the Devil card, and I don't really like knowing their names, though sometimes it's unavoidable. It's better when they're just meat. I mean, you don't name the cows you make hamburgers out of, am I right?"

I felt nauseous at her analogy, but I kept going. It was after midnight, and I'd been there for a while already, but I felt the situation was gaining momentum. I wanted to finish this and stop coming here to hear these terrible things. I wanted Catherine Meara to pay for what she'd done. I was impatient for justice to be served, and something inside me knew the black eyes she wore hinted at impending doom.

"Okay," I said, getting her details straight. "After you killed the blonde, you left. You told her you were headed for Mechanicsburg. Was that true?"

"Absolutely. I needed a Tower, and Philly was too far away to make it in time. Besides, the raven I needed for the Tower was hard at work, building his nest in Mechanicsburg. I had the perfect building, and raven, in mind and I couldn't wait to get there."

"You knew the next victim beforehand? You didn't find them at random?"

"Sophia, really. You act like I'm this unorganized freak. Yes, when the opportunity presents itself, I'll take advantage like any hunter. I'm a planner at heart. You might say the whole project, my tribute to the dark lord, began with the seed of an idea involving the raven whose manner of sacrifice was chosen by the Tower card. A wicked little raven named Damien Edwards."

16-The Tower

Something nagged the back of my brain, a fleeting memory, but I couldn't hold it firmly in my grasp. Finally, I said, "Okay, I'll bite. Who is Damien Edwards and why was he an 'evil raven' destined to die on the Tower?"

"Aw, you almost had it," she clucked sympathetically. "You probably read about it in the papers since you're not big time enough to cover such a story on your own. But...if you cast back far enough, you might remember him from high school."

At those words, memory broke through the fog and shattered into a thousand fragments. I remembered a tall young man, mocha skin gleaming with health under the stadium lights. A football hero, I recalled, handsome and popular, skimming the hallways of the high school with the ease of a person who is having the time of his life. I was a book worm, mostly, a loner. His polar opposite. He was a few years older than me too, but he was always nice to me. I remembered that with painful clarity.

More memories swam to the surface, like koi darting to kiss the air in a pond. He and a younger version of Catherine holding hands in the halls. Him insisting they sit at my table during lunch. His white teeth contrasting so beautifully with his dark skin as he smiled at me, asking about the book I was reading. So earnest, trying so hard to include me. And Catherine, staring off into space, bored, or staring at me with her weird eyes like I was a specimen in a Petri dish.

"Damien," I whispered. Another memory of Damien danced outside my conscious mind, teasing.

"Wasn't he pretty?" Catherine's black stare somehow felt the same as it had that day in the cafeteria, long ago.

"What did you do to him?" I demanded.

"Back then? Nothing. I tried to give myself to him actually, but he rejected me! He said he wasn't ready and I shouldn't be either. That we should save ourselves for love! Can you believe that? I told him he would be sorry one day that we were finished, and he should watch his back!

"He said he felt sorry for me because I had no parents and my grandparents didn't pay attention to me. I said he could take his pity and shove it up his ass! After the day he refused to touch me, I vowed no man would ever touch me. When Damien rejected me, I focused all my energy on pleasing the Goddess. It still wasn't enough. Never enough! She feels that fertility is important and had no use for a woman who vowed to remain a pure vessel! What did she know, anyway? I had so much more power when I came to the dark lord because I abstained from using my energy on breeding. He deemed that, from then on, he would be my only lover and I have never regretted it once."

"Not even once, Catherine? What about the beautiful boy you ran over with his own car?"

She sat back in her chair, cocky and at ease for the first time in a while. She didn't acknowledge my comment, or her moment of weakness. "I found Damien a couple of years ago on the Internet," she said instead. "He turned out to be an architect, which surprised me. All I ever heard was football but of course, that was a long time ago. I'd wanted to get even for a long time too, so I started planning. Finally, around the first week of September, right after the blond bimbo, I contacted him via email to see if he wanted to get together for dinner sometime. He seemed really pleased to hear from me, and we exchanged phone numbers. I set up a meeting for dinner on September 22nd for about eight p.m. and it was Damien who suggested we meet at the Tower Room restaurant in Harrisburg. I took that as a good omen, the name of the place. Have you been there?"

"Oh my God, the Tower Room," I breathed. I remembered where else I had heard Damien's name before. Damien Edwards, age twenty nine, had been found on the crumpled hood of a parked Prius on the street below the Tower Room restaurant on September 22nd, 2012. At the time I'd read about the incident, the name nagged at me but I had been unable to place it. Damien was older, and the memory of his kindness had faded along with his name over time.

"The police never figured out if he had jumped or been pushed," I recalled the details of the story. "The other diners and the wait staff reported he was there with a woman, but no one could agree on any details, like hair color or clothing. The police were toying with the idea that the entire restaurant had been drugged somehow, to make up for the lack of cohesive eyewitness testimony."

Catherine grinned. "Pays to have an edge. Don't you think?"

"Did you push him out the window?"

"No, I didn't. Those windows didn't open, they were fixed. I am not strong enough to shove a strapping fellow like Damien out through the glass with my puny little girl arms." She held up her arms, encased in the blue prison uniform, for emphasis. Her handcuffs rattled and clinked. "Besides he paid for his mistake in scorning me so what's the difference how he ended up as a hood ornament?"

"But...what about the ritual? How does his death count as the Tower card if you didn't sacrifice him correctly?"

"Very good!" she said approvingly. "We may teach you yet! You're right. It wouldn't have counted but he was late getting to the restaurant and I specifically requested a table near the window in a secluded area, hinting how we needed an intimate setting. Wink wink. I cast the circle around the table after the waiter brought me our waters, just before Damien showed up, handsome as ever. I had to draw the raven in my blood on his chair, making sure to cut myself somewhere discreet where he wouldn't notice. Not optimal, as the symbol should really be drawn on the sacrifice's chest but it was the best I could do. My blood was technically on him, which was good enough. I made sure I was a sufficient distraction and he was so busy looking at me he never noticed his bloody chair before he sat down. As for how he got through that window…well, I think I'll keep some secrets for myself.

"I set my sights for home after that. I took Damien's keys to his black Mercedes and hightailed it. I knew the cops would be busy extracting him from the roof of the Prius he'd demolished. I figured I'd ditch the Merc after a visit to the old homestead, where dear old granny, my Cadillac, and another little taste of payback waited for me."

"Your grandmother is still alive?" I asked, surprised.

Again, I was awarded that mischievous smile I knew so well. "Well, not anymore."

17-The Star

My granny was young when she whelped my mother," the witch explained. "So the old bird was about eighty-nine when I finally came back home. I wish I could say she was happy to see me, but..."

"Did she know? Did she feel responsible for unleashing you on the world? Or was she completely clueless as to what you were?"

"Oh she knew. Granny Meara was about as Irish as they come, more Irish than that sexy cop you're banging. Just as Catholic as your grandmother was, too. No sense of pagan and Catholic overlap in my life, though, unlike yours. Grandpa was pretty superstitious but he always got smacked every time he made the evil eye at me. She'd whack him with her wooden stirring spoon and say, 'Blasphemer!' with that fire and brimstone look in her eye.

One time, after my parents died in a 'horrible fire'," Catherine mocked, making quotation marks in the air with her bound hands, "my granny got it into her head that I'd barbecued them. She called in her priest, who she worshipped like he was Jesus himself, and tried to exorcise my demons. And guess what?"

"What?" I asked, sickened.

The deep, booming voice erupted from her delicate throat again, roaring, "It didn't work!" She/it laughed, a sound that echoed through the prison like thunder.

Brad's radio crackled with urgent voices. I heard the word 'riot' and Brad shouting orders to contain it. He turned to his two officers, pointing into the cell and shouting, "Don't leave them alone!" and took off down the hall at a run with the other officer at his heels.

I turned back to Catherine, who was wearing her Mona Lisa cat smile again, eyes as black as ink pools.

In her normal voice she said, "I drowned granny in the bathtub. She pulled the Star card. Fitting, for someone who was so pious. I enjoyed listening to her recite the

Lord's Prayer over and over while I cast the circle around the bathtub and drew the raven on her wrinkly chest. She was light as a raven too, as if her bones were hollow. It didn't take her long to die. I was almost disappointed but I guess she would be the best sacrifice I could make for the Star card. She did die in fear, one of its meanings, but I'd hoped for something a bit more spectacular. Maybe a showdown between good and evil or something. The dark lord said nothing, for once, about my sacrifice to him. But like they say, no news is good news so I went ahead with it."

"You are a monster, you really are. How can you talk about killing your family so easily, without feeling?"

Her black eyes gleamed. "What did they ever do for me? NOTHING! Except DIE so I could honor the one being who ever TRULY CARED!" she shouted, the cords in her neck standing out in stark relief beneath the single light bulb.

I shouted back. "You're so predictable, spouting about that dark lord shit, and woe is me nobody ever loved me. It's all BULLSHIT! Let me guess...next you loaded up the Caddy and hauled ass off to your next killing ground, right? There is NOTHING to back up what you are saying Catherine. I think you are LYING!"

She was immediately calm, another flip of the switch. "Of course you don't. And not exactly, no, I did not just head for my next killing ground. I spent a few months in Philly, researching you. The ravens love you, you know."

I was sickened. "You followed me?"

"Oh yes! I needed to get to know you. I never bothered when we were kids but then I read your article, on the same day I found Damien as a matter of fact. I was fascinated so I decided to come find you. To my surprise you turned out to be quite interesting."

"Interesting now?"

"Well, you tell stories for a living, for one thing. And your power! It's rough, really raw, but so plentiful. I only touched you for a moment yesterday, but siphoned off enough of your power so that not only have you not noticed its lack but I'm still completely overcharged. You're like...a witch battery! How I wish we were on the same side," she lamented.

"I will never be as fucked up as you are, Catherine, no matter what your 'dark lord' mutters in that sick brain of yours."

The wind howled through the tiny cell again, whistling in the high ceiling and swirling around the two of us. That was my only warning before she launched herself over the table at me, hands curved into claws, reaching for my throat. The officer at the door leaped in front of me a split second before she got to me, his reflexes much better than my own. It was very brave and also the last thing he ever did.

18-The Moon

She ripped his throat out with her fingers and flung bits of gore and flesh to the ground. As if they were strings, Catherine broke her handcuffs apart and raised her arms to the ceiling, laughing. She touched the shackles on her legs and they fell away, the smoking and melted metal sending charred ozone smells into the air.

"Well, there goes number sixteen," she boomed in her demon's voice. "I was hoping to have your sexy cop instead, but I guess one dead pig is as tasty as the next."

I was tied fast in my chair by invisible ropes of her power, unable to move or flee from her approaching form. She stood before me, ink black eyes blazing evil into my soul. Her flame colored hair twisted around her head like snakes in the wind, lazy and aimless. She grinned at me, drool leaking from the corner of her mouth and dribbling onto the floor as she grabbed the dead officer by his legs and pulled him to the corner of the room near the cot.

"I call upon the guardians in the North, guided by Air;
I call upon the guardians in the South, guided by Fire;
I call upon the guardians in the West, guided by Water;
I call upon the guardians in the East, guided by Earth.
I enter the circle in the name of the Horned God,
And I come to do his bidding!"

At the end of her incantation, a crimson light flashed in a circle around her and the officer's body, glowing with otherworldly power. It mesmerized me with its glow, so unlike anything I'd ever seen before. She brought her right wrist to her lips and tore the flesh with her teeth, blood oozing over the edges of her ripped skin to drip in quick patterns on the cement floor. She tore open the officer's uniform shirt and with deft motions, drew the raven on his still warm body. She made a cutting motion in the portion of the glowing circle nearest to me, and the light faded, went out.

Her attention turned back to me, and she whispered a singsong chant as she came nearer, weaving back and forth in a strange, snakelike dance. Her face had changed, the teeth elongated and features harsh, more pointed; her eyes were still inky pools of darkness but with a crimson glow beneath them, like an eclipsed pair of suns leaking from her eye sockets. As I watched, they bubbled over, black slime oozing from her eye sockets as though they had been filled with metal, now molten and flowing down her face like lava. Black feathers sprouted from her flesh, tearing through her prison uniform in sprays of blood, springing from her scalp to mingle with her flame hair. Talons tore from her fingers, curving and flexing in the air as she reveled in her transformation. She opened her mouth to scream her triumph and what emerged was not the booming demonic voice of before, nor her musical siren's voice, but rather the harsh caw of a raven, magnified a hundredfold.

I screamed in fear, in rage, in loathing and she laughed her insane asylum howling at me.

Brad hurtled himself into the cell, gun blazing as he fired round after round at the thing that was Catherine. The bullets pierced her, the impact flinging her against the concrete wall of the cell, but she didn't stop. Instead, she kept coming forward, only now her attention was on Brad instead of me, and she reached him fast, so fast, driving her taloned fingers into his stomach and lifting him up into the air. She flung him with inhuman strength against the opposite cell wall. As he lay there, stunned and bleeding, she pointed a clawed hand at him and levitated him into the air, some elemental force or power rocketing through her

and at the man I loved, hurling him against the concrete
again and again before she grew tired and let him slide
down its slick surface, trailing blood in thick swatches,
until he finally came to rest in a crumpled heap on the floor.

19-The Sun

It was as though all of the sunlight was sucked from my life and narrowed down to that one instant, where my eyes met Brad's through a haze of blood and pain. I saw him mouth the words, "I love you," before the light dimmed from his eyes and he saw me no more.

In that instant, I became my destiny. There was no god, gods, or goddesses to help me against the Raven Witch. There was only me. I closed my eyes on the sight of her reaching for Brad's body, no doubt intending to cast her circle and desecrate his flesh with her polluted blood. I reached deep inside of myself and found that thing, that gift or power or whatever it should be named, and I pulled it forth to examine it more closely. I saw how my oath of love to Brad had been fulfilled, and part of me rejoiced while the other part mourned his loss. I shoved all that aside and concentrated on finding what would defeat her. I found it, swirling in the center of all emotion, the one pure thing, the one true thing, even she could not deny.

I opened my eyes and found her looming over me. Whatever she saw gave her a pause, the feathers on her shoulders ruffling uneasily, just as a bird's does when they settle their feathers into place. "What are you doing, Sophia?" her harsh voice cawed.

Now my voice held all the music in the world when I replied, "I see you Catherine. I see the real you, all your tricks and spells are ripped away. I embrace my power for what it is. I know who and what I am now. All life is just energy and yours is wasted on you."

I thrust my power into her, no need to touch her foul flesh with my own, and her raven's body writhed in agony. The feathers were stripped from her as though a giant hand grasped them and ripped them away, pulling her disguise off like one sheds their clothes at the end of the day. She screamed in fury, now just a beautiful woman with rotting insides.

"You can only be what you truly are," I told her. I slowed time around me, playing with it as though it were a new toy, mine to command. She resisted my power, using her own powers to fling bolts of energy at me, but I absorbed them with ease, ramping up my own power until I was all but humming with it. For her last trick, she produced the Sun card like a magician, flinging it at my face where it opened a cut beneath my cheek. She turned from me and fled from the cell, her first taste of freedom in many days. She ran down the hall as I walked behind her. She glanced over her shoulder to see how close I was, and hit the hub with a bolt of power and electricity, opening the gates while the guards reacted in slow motion thanks to my time manipulation. I followed her relentlessly, my walking pace as fast as her running could carry her, my power carrying me forward of its own accord, and she hit the front doors hard, spinning out into the sunlight of the newly risen morning.

She lifted her face, the beautiful face with the newly restored blue-green splotched eyes, to the sun. I believe Catherine could have been a good witch, if she had chosen to follow the path of the light rather than the sickening sweet whisper of a false god. Her hair shone in the morning sun like a newly minted copper penny. I watched to see what she would do, protected from her by the bulletproof glass doors and my own heady power.

She turned to the front gates, where seventeen ravens now waited for her. Seventeen, one for each person she killed. I knew there was one for the officer who had saved me, and one for the man I loved who had done the same, but I couldn't think of that now. I had judgment to pass.

The guards at the front gates were slowed by my

time manipulation, but they saw her smile at the birds and move toward the gates. The largest of them let loose a coughing caw sound, spurring the others to beat the air with their wings. I did not hear them, but saw the guards cover their ears with their time slowed hands, guns forgotten in the immediacy of their pained expressions.

Catherine passed through the gates unimpeded, sparing no further glance for her feathery host. From far and wide, animals of every sort could be seen gathering around the edges of the prison, from small creatures like birds, mice, and squirrels to larger animals like foxes, deer, and even a pair of wolves from who knew where. The other guards later said they saw nothing but the pit, though I saw the animals and thought it fitting.

She stepped through the wrought iron gates and turned back to smile at me for the last time. It held so much promise that smile. It spoke of triumph and gloating, but also sadness and apology. I had reached my verdict, however.

I raised my hand and made a circular motion, gathering all the forces I possessed. Like stirring a pot of stew, I circled over and over, eyes closed in concentration, so that I felt, rather than saw, the earth beneath Catherine's feet swirl like the tornado of water, like the water spout that forms when a drain is pulled in a bathtub. My mind's eye saw her terror and her relief as judgment was passed on her by the only peer she recognized. The earth took her, swallowed her up like a delectable treat. Only when I felt her die, when I felt her energy absorbed by the very earth that created her, did I open my eyes to view the destruction I'd wrought. I saw, in a daze, the Sun tarot card floating lazily downward to land at my feet, sent from who knows where. The Sun, meant to symbolize happiness. That was when the tears finally came.

20-Judgement

Officially, Catherine Meara died of natural causes, a burst blood vessel in the brain, most likely a result of her trip into the sinkhole. Experts explained that the entire area around the prison had once been coal mining country. Coal mining caused the sinkhole that pulled Catherine Meara into the ground, where she died of an aneurism caused by the shock and distress of the situation. It took them an entire day to pull her body from the ground. An entire day for me to sit, empty and hollow, on the now familiar prison steps and watch the ravens fly away, one by one.

I was allowed to read a copy of the coroner's report. I think he felt sorry for me. I didn't need stitches on my face where Catherine's Sun card cut me, but the bruised and swollen areas of my face and body helped foster the image of a brutal beating victim. I was silent about the true events of that night and morning at Pennsylvania State Penitentiary. I claimed it was too confused and blurred for me to remember, citing emotional trauma as a contributing factor. The last part was even true. I remembered watching them bring Brad's body out on a stretcher, covered with a white sheet, stained with blood. His hand peeked through the side closest to me and I had the overwhelming urge to touch it as it went by me. I didn't. Brad wasn't in there anymore, his energy gone on to something or somewhere else. I felt it lingering close by, and was afraid for him.

The notation of Catherine's marks on her body in the coroner's report did not include the raven tattoos flying across her back from shoulder to shoulder. I knew why they were gone. The first one showed up on my shoulder, upon her death, and I knew its friends would follow shortly behind it.

I went home to the Philly Herald. Rick put me on Entertainment and I gladly filled my little sections of text with silly nothings and meaningless prattle. The inane nature of it all soothed me. I did not sleep at night, any more. I slept in the day time and showed up at the office around five each evening. Rick even gave me a raise, and sometimes stayed behind after hours to have a drink and try to cheer me up. He was a good man.

It was from him that I learned more about the aftermath of the events at the prison. After Catherine's death, Dayne Yoakum and another County Sherriff named Sam Johnson had put their heads, and information, together and came up with a list of possible bodies and missing persons. All of them fit the descriptions of her victims in Brad's notes, found on his desk and on his body at the coroner's office.

I claimed my recordings were lost and did not elaborate on the information they located, but they didn't need me. The two lovers in Clinton County were never found, but James White was located in Luzerne County, as was the body of Melissa Anselme in an abandoned warehouse on the outskirts of Williamsport. The pieces of her body, that is. They'd searched over thirty such buildings before finding what was left of her, bones and bits of flesh further ravaged by time, rats, and insects.

Edward Garretty was finally located as well, by backpackers trying to find themselves in the wilderness. When they lost track of their supply caches and became lost in the woods, they viewed the appearance of a seemingly abandoned cabin as manna from heaven. They changed their minds when they found Mr. Garretty's body strapped to the bed, mouth open in a rictus of eternal screaming. When they found civilization, they pointed local police in Tioga County to the general direction of the cabin so he could receive a proper burial.

Finnaeus Parsons, the history guy, was found in his charred home but police never knew who'd set the fire until they were contacted by Sheriffs Johnson and Yoakum in connection with Catherine Meara. Autopsy reports revealed Mr. Parsons had been tortured extensively before being doused with accelerant and set on fire. The report also revealed he was still alive before the flames finally consumed him. Catherine had lied about that one.

The bodies of the infant, Mary the Hanged Man victim, and the two hunters in Sugarcreek still had not been found but some names were connected to the disappearances. Jules and Verne Fields, aged forty, were unrecoverable, their house incinerated so completely that only their teeth and bits of bone remained to identify them. Police assumed their death was accidental, a leaking gas line or some such thing, but reopened the case once contacted by Yoakum.

The blonde in the port-a-potty was recovered and found to be a missing woman from a good home in Huntingdon County. Wendy Rossman, mother of two and wife to Chet Rossman, went missing in early August of 2012. After dropping her kids off at school, she simply vanished, taking nothing with her as far as her husband could tell. No one had the heart to tell him she'd been dressed like a hooker and off to find adventure when she met Catherine Meara instead. Sherriff Johnson delivered the news to him personally, holding the big man like a baby when he cried.

The death of Damien Edwards was well documented, but no one could figure out how he'd managed to break through those giant plate glass windows, until the events at the prison. Those of us who saw what Catherine was capable of kept it to ourselves but after Brad's death, and the death of the other officers, no one doubted she'd killed Damien somehow as well.

Imogene Meara's death had been ruled an accident. An old woman, living alone, drowning in the bathtub...it was not far-fetched. Her death is now attributed to the Raven Witch Killer as well. Catherine killed where she had been given life, a roof over her head, and a chance to become something.

Officer Allan DeGroot, aged thirty-six had given his life to protect mine. And of course, so did Officer Bradley Shaw. I tried not to think about him too much. I tried.

I didn't eat much, and most of what I did eat came back up. My dreams were empty.

It wasn't until exactly seventeen days after the incident in the prison that the first raven showed up on the window ledge of my apartment, though its image was imbedded in the flesh on my back and shoulders. Seventeen times, of course. We stared at each other, but neither of us said anything. The bird was carrying the Judgment card in its ebony beak. The bird let the card fall, but it was picked up by the wind and floated away in a complicated dance, where some person may have found it on a sidewalk, picked it up, and never known its true significance. I'd made my Judgment back at the prison.

I went to a Tarot card reader, once, out of curiosity. The woman tried too hard to be 'New Age', wearing her version of hippie clothes and her house reeked of incense. When I sat down and she began to read my cards, she grew more and more distressed as the session stretched on. She finally refused to read for me, and would say no more. I paid her anyway.

I spent hours in the dark switching the lamp on and off with my power, which I no longer hid from. I hoped the lamplight would chase away the demons in the shadows. I spent many hours conjuring Brad's image from trails of energy only to have them to dissipate and leave me feeling desolate once again.

I would've continued on this way for some time had I not finally figured out what the ravens wanted of me and why I felt as though I was not completely alone in spite of the absence of the man I'd pledged my soul to. Through the fog of my depression there was a voice in the darkness that gave me strength.

The next day, there were two ravens. And then three. And so on. We spent many hours silently contemplating each other. I began to draw them, investing in sketch pads and expensive charcoal pencils. I grew intimately familiar with the anatomy of ravens, researching them constantly, from their wedge shaped tail feathers to their shaggy neck feathers. I collected their elongated primary feathers from the ledge outside my window and glued them to my drawings.

Every day, I slept, ate, vomited, and drew the ravens. I dreamed nothing. I began hanging the drawings on my walls until they were covered with endless images of ravens. I no longer left the house, having food delivered and emailing Rick my pieces for the paper.

Always, there were ravens out on the window ledge, endlessly watching me. One of them was larger than the others. It stayed through night and day, never taking any sustenance that I saw. I spent every moment obsessing about them, wondering if they were hers, come to finish me as she'd intended. Or worse, maybe they were mine, now.

Then I found out why they were really there.

21-The World

The story is told, finally. That was the last piece of what was required of me and the weight upon my shoulders will leave...eventually. I have drawn the World card, and it has come to signal the end.

The ravens have gone. All but the largest one, who still visits. That one is mine.

I've lost so much already. I will not sacrifice the child in my womb on the altar of Catherine's evil legacy.

As I will it, so mote it be.

<u>About the Author:</u>

Chrystal (Christina) Vaughan lives in the Pacific Northwest with her family. When she is not writing, she likes to impart her love for the written word to others and is a voracious reader.

"A Conspiracy of Ravens" is Mrs. Vaughan's third novel; other books from this author include "Sideshow" and "Dead in the Water" (a Solstice Publishing title). Both are available at Amazon and Barnes and Noble.

Comments can be directed to the author at mermaidsandmayhem@gmail.com or visit her on Facebook at: https://www.facebook.com/chrystalwrites

Other methods of contact include Twitter (@TheChrystalShip), or visit her blog at www.mermaidsandmayhem.blogspot.com for previews and excerpts from upcoming books!

<u>Acknowledgements:</u>

I dedicated this book to my husband, and here's why: for putting up with the light on in bed through all hours of the night while I scribbled, for accepting answers half murmured in response to questions not fully heard, and for letting me just be me, a crazy writer.

I'd also like to acknowledge my children, one of whom listened to bits of plot until she had to plug her ears and say, "No no no! I'm going to read this one, don't tell me anymore!" and also crafted the amazing cover; the other child reminded me of my real job by saying, "Mom, stop writing, it's time to snuggle."

A big thanks to my proofreader, mother, and cheerleader, Dee Teaford; my beta reader and cheerleader, Annette Williams; and to my test readers and cheerleaders Dayna Clark, Heather Tramp, Chris Rajnus, Laura Nolte, Gianna Row and Kymri Butcher. (Kymri, I'm sorry the serial killer in this book looked like you...it was an accident I swear!). Thanks to my editor Sherry Derr-Wille and my editor-in-chief KC Sprayberry, and my Solstice family for their support.

I'd like to thank all my family and friends who read my books and support my writing. You all know who you are.

Finally, thanks to my students. They know why.

www.ingramcontent.com/pod-product-compliance
Lightning Source LLC
Chambersburg PA
CBHW051344020726
47501CB00007B/2261